Permit My American Dream

Two Sides To Every Coin

By

Vernon Augustus Brooks

ISBN 978-0-6151-7062-6

Permit My American Dream

Two Sides To Every Coin

Edited

By

Vernon Augustus Brooks

ABOUT THE AUTHOR

Vernon Augustus Brooks was born on May 27, 1960 in the district of Danvers Pen, St. Thomas, Jamaica. His late parents, Gertrude Elizabeth Barrant and Henry Nicholas Brooks influenced him from very early in his life to prioritize education. He made them proud in 1972 when he gained a scholarship to attend Morant Bay High School, where he later debuted his teaching profession at the tender age of 19.

*During his stint as a scholar, he was actively involved in track and field athletics, a feat that he continued while reading for the Bachelor of Arts and Master of Science degrees at the University of the West Indies (UWI), from 1981 to 1990. Over the years, Vernon Augustus Brooks contributed to education, teaching at schools in the following locations: **Jamaica** - Morant Bay High School, St. Hugh's High School, Kingston College, Kingston Technical High School, St. Thomas Technical High School, The Queen's High School, Jamaica College, EXED Community College (Evening); **British Virgin Islands (BVI)** - Anegada Secondary High School, Bregado Flax Educational Center (Secondary Division); **Netherlands Antilles** - Saba Comprehensive High School; **United Kingdom** - West Hertz College; **USA** - Play and Learn Academy, Bergen County College of Advancement Training(BCCAT)/Felician College.*

He has taught eleven subjects in spanning the above-mentioned institutions. They are randomly: Spanish, French, English Language, English Literature, History, Geography, Economics, Social

Studies, Psychology, English as a Second Language (ESL), Drama. The levels include Caribbean Examination Council (CXC), General Certificate of Education (GCE) Advanced Level, GCE Ordinary Level, and college education.

Vernon Augustus Brooks continued his education in England, completing an MA degree in Counseling Studies at the University of Derby. While he plans to do doctoral studies in the near future, he has committed himself to writing a few short books, and has already started the flow with (1) Tricks And Trades Of The Jamaican Man, (2) Mysteries And Myths About Married Men and (3) Teacher-Student Trysts: Coping With A Kiddy Crush. He is aspiring to restore the flawlessness that used to be characteristic of writing, and therefore hopes to get the recognition he deserves.

ACKNOWLEDGEMENT

I wish to express my appreciation for the assistance I received from Mr. Dominik Kozubal, who used his competence in computer technology to arrange the title to match the cover of this book. I reserve my sincerest regards for his input.

CONTENTS...PAGES

INTRODUCTION

Thinking Twice In Paradise

As a Jamaican who lives and works in the USA, I find it rather interesting that when I tell strangers what it feels like, to frolic in a river in the land of my origin, or even to pick up a sun-ripened mango, oozing at its stubby stem after it falls from a tree in that land of wood, fruits and water, people from other continents quickly call that paradise. Yet this compliment is coming from the mouth of travelers who left their countries in search of a better life. And if while they are at the spot believed to be the *Promised Land*, they think Jamaica is a taste of heaven, then we ought to appreciate what we have more than anyone else.

Get this straight, not one river in the US is ideal for swimming or bathing, unless the plunge is a suicidal attempt. The rivers are so polluted that if somebody should cautiously test the waters with his foot, his main toe would perhaps disappear like it was dipped in a sea of concentrated hydrochloric acid. And a sun-ripened mango! Maybe in Miami, but elsewhere, that's like searching for a needle in a haystack.

However, Jamaicans believe that paradise is the place to which all roads lead in the modern world, and that is speaking of the United States of America. The perhaps undisputable fact, of which the unexposed population of this minute country is still unaware, is that the grass is always greener on the other side. And there are millions of Americans who would love to trade places with Jamaicans. While countless aspirants are eager to dig up roots and go to the USA, there are so many from Uncle Sam's sanctuary, who would love to breathe some fresh air, and take a dip in our rivers every now and again, but can't fulfill their wish to switch lifestyles.

It's only when many Jamaicans migrate to America, they get a good look at the unfair exchange in terms of landscape. And by then, they would have burnt their bridges behind them, so they simply stick to the evil they already know. Those who don't travel will never be convinced by those who do, because the social psychology that has already been circulated is that the USA is indeed the center stage of world - *God Bless America*! Only when an incident like the New Orleans crisis is shown on satellite, some might be tempted to believe their eyes. And in a matter of days, the disaster is quickly forgotten and so is the social reality.

In ***Permit My American Dream: Two Sides To Every Coin***, Bruce Welds had been hearing so much about America since his childhood, during which, farm workers and other migrants painted a beautiful picture of the safe haven. In his adult life, he uprooted to pursue his American dream on a visiting visa that he got on his third attempt at the famous US Embassy in Oxford Road, Kingston. Entering through Puerto Rico, an American property in the Caribbean, he found himself in Bronx, New York, before struggling to survive in Wethersfield, Connecticut. Then it was back to Bronx, like he was being tossed up and down and all around on a *Bounce About Jumper*, against his will in other people's entertainment park.

Bruce vigorously chased his tail, enduring racism and prejudice at times painfully encompassed in veiled forms of institutionalized discrimination. The other minority immigrants told similar stories, and he definitely took it personal. He wanted to return home, but his situation forced him to grin and bear. He could only stay put, and wished to send a clear message to his countrymen that they should look before they leapt, so that they enjoyed their paradise while they still had the power.

The story develops along a series that's certainly not chronological and consequently, the narrative technique uses flashbacks, narration, cinematographic snapshots and incidents to get the plot rolling. There is a mosaic pattern piloted by the protagonist's stream of consciousness, and time is of the essence in the occasional breaks between the paragraphs.

The plot is choppy, so it also determines the characters and their presentation. Readers should encounter mainly character-types rather than well-rounded individuals, and they are introduced along the way as the circumstances arise. One exception is Bruce, who is the narrator and also the protagonist. Hence, one inevitably meets him from the beginning, getting to know that he used to live in suburban Kingston, albeit a product of St. Thomas in the eastern coast of Jamaica. Since he leads the way in the cast, all eyes are on his movement as he takes the crowd from place to place. Meanwhile, his observers don't know what to expect from the erratic composition of the occurrences that seem to be guided by fate.

A few of the antagonists (those who are mean or only help to stir up trouble for the traveler), are thrown in from out of nowhere, and their identities are either noted because of a nameplate, their position of authority or their frictional nature. These include Miguel in CHAPTER TWO and Hilary in CHAPTER SIX, or even Jenny and Pam in CHAPTER FOUR. There are other personnel who appear and disappear soon after, while some stick around longer than others. There are also those who have a permanent place in the narrator's memory like Kenny and Myra, as well as Bev, Dawn and Faith. Some turn up again in reference to familiar incidents to provide moral support. For example, a reader couldn't be surprised if the narrator should speak of the devil, and Rick's name reappeared, long after his exit, as a case of clarification or comparison. Reiteratively, the incidents that are brought in to contribute to the reality of the story are short-lived, and therefore the characters stick around only as long as their roles are current.

The setting is also reflected in the movement of the plot and the incidents that incite the narrative. For instance, one minute the reader could be in an airplane, floating on the narrator's stream of consciousness that travels back to the protagonist's own childhood. Then the next second, the scene may quickly shift to somewhere more immediate, or closer to reality, like in Wethersfield or Bronx. There's no guarantee that any one particular scene is going to be revisited on account of the erratic nature of the plot.

The names of the places are those that actually exist, and this in itself contributes to the true-to-life adherence of the narrative. Gun Hill Road and Wethersfield are on the map, and a reader can always identify with the characteristics of these locations to get the vividness that's originally intended. A little geography is imparted in the process of capturing the details behind the scenes, and this helps to keep things fresh in any reader's mind.

The style of the literature is basically conventional with regular usage of figures of speech and literary devices such as clichés, imageries, personifications, contrasts, hyperboles, etc. However, these are the strands that stitch the work together to give it some fictional qualities, in as much as the realism starkly overpowers it to present a contrary picture. The language makes use of many American spellings throughout the coverage*.

Speaking of realism, this has a very significant spot in the development of the story. Usually, a fictional tale that tinkers with this art of presentation makes a concerted effort to employ authenticity, to pepper the preponderant imaginative ingredients. In ***Permit My American Dream: Two Sides To Every Coin***, it's the other way around to portray a true story - concrete characters driven by familiar conflicts in proper places known all over the world. Hence, apart from the prevalence of toponyms (place-names), a surrealistic report like the pigeon passing its poops in the wrong place when Bruce was right on time, is not uncommon.

And those who know New York can readily visualize these doves in their verifiable dynasty, shooting their loads wherever nature calls. Hence, when the same thing happened to Bruce, as one strange face in the crowd walking on 42nd Street, he must have wondered "why me?" But so would just about anybody in real life, if that individual became the one in a million, for something that nasty to target.

Contrasting events also canvass for realism, and might even be a difference between life and death. In CHAPTER TWO, Pat left the BVI to bring her newborn into the world in St. Thomas of the US Virgin Islands. Conversely, Rod was robbed of his life at a very untimely hour, when the girl he only just met, sank the blade of a kitchen knife into his heart.

The differences of the details are sometimes as distinct as day and night, sadness and jubilation. The night that Bruce found himself at Rick's ranch in Wethersfield was like being in the doldrums, nothing compared to the good times Carlton created on sunny Saturdays for folks in the reggae country, when Bruce was young. Similarly, Bruce was the happiest man on the face of the earth when he got that stamp in his passport, but the feeling was reversed when acts of discrimination stared him in the face in the land of opportunities.

There are a few sub-themes that stand out for avid observation. Superstition was not spared when the narrator detailed his dreams that usually occurred ahead of an adventure. The bee that bit Bruce as a wake-up call that his true luck was about to begin, is an omen fit for assimilation in fortune-telling forums. The bird that hopped, skipped and jumped to lead the way to lost cash that might have otherwise been kept hidden in the bushes, gives a new meaning to coincidence, if a reader is tempted to write off Bruce's encounter as a similar sort. The nightingale that was the nuisance of the neighborhood in the wee hours of the morning, initiates the idea to make animals the ominous mascots in this literary equation.

Prejudice is another piece of the puzzle to find the main threads that link the plot. The woman in the line to get the visa at Oxford Road expressed preference to face a male consulate, but she might have gotten the notion that nothing was straightforward, when giving the devil his dues. The women in that Wethersfield episode had their own vision of a black guy, and nothing was going to change that, even if a good one from the Caribbean stepped up in their faces. And as Bruce lived to discover, that side of the world might have developed the symptoms from some other places in the whole USA.

The main theme is relevant to the title, ***Permit My American Dream: Two Sides To Every Coin***, which articulates every facet throughout the novel. It's in pursuit of the American dream that Bruce, like millions of Jamaicans, competed for documentation in *The States*, only to live to think twice in paradise. The protagonist's proven track record in traveling extended to the British Virgin Islands, a move which might seem remote in any connection to this thematic network. However, St. Thomas in the proximate US Virgin Islands gave him a glimpse of the hype that augmented the urges of many islanders to try for the mainland.

People, like Pat, crossed rough seas in faulty ferries to give birth just so that kids there could get a chance at life among the lucky ones in the long run. Those who came from outer places were willing to put their freedom at risk, buying birth-papers even when their accents gave them away. These catalysts promoted the push and pull factors that circulated the psychology of settling in America.

This introduction conclusively leaves the reader to decipher the rest of the intriguing features of the story. It's like watching a film and a viewer could do with some exposition to clear the way. However, the last thing a zealous moviegoer needs is for someone who is still ecstatic about the contents of the movie, to spill the beans of the scenes to water down the suspense. Hence, without further ado, it is time to delve into the density of this context, and get familiar with the data firsthand.

American spelling/usage: color, traveler, traveling, check (meaning money), story (meaning floor of a building), practice (as verb), license (as noun)

CHAPTER ONE

It's Not Unusual To Dream Big

"*The Big Apple*, here I come! Move over Donald Trump, time's up!" The big league guys came to mind.

I must have been bursting at the seams with delightful optimism while reacting to my good fortune, on the day that I managed to elude all odds to secure the coveted stamp in my passport. The positive patch of words that read, "United States of America Visa", was stylistically etched squarely on a selected page of the national blue book that reiteratively claimed its ownership by the Jamaican government in fine print. The universal gold spoon bore close resemblance to the almighty dollar in terms of color and background.

That insignia must have been the most significant entry, among the clusters of evidence that other countries branded in my booklet, to show that I had increased their population at some point. I felt as though this signature statement held me up like the burning torch in the hand of *The Statue of Liberty*. Importantly, I had been set free to begin the quest of my American dream, something that billions around the world craved every minute that they took the breath of life for granted.

In my mirror I saw the start of great things, considering that the land of opportunities indirectly propositioned me to come. My future was already written in the skies, and not even the green-eyed monster living next to me could get the better of this breakthrough, not over my 34-year-old, living body. Like a dolphin in the deep, I had always believed that what was mine could not be for someone else, and that had simply become my monumental motto.

I thought I was unstoppable, futuristically relying on this change for the better to bestow all the best on my total longevity.

Every single scratch had some meaning that deserved to be discovered, and I tried to reconcile my new calling with everything that ever happened under my keen observation; little things which suggested that my day would eventually come. Plus, my horoscope for one particular week was packed with tremendous news that my lucky stars revealed generously and frequently, to those with a second pair of eyes.

"The gurus were so right," I commended, talking to the air as I drifted on the memory.

Two nights before the unforgettable day that the American consulate exercised his extremely rare and random discretion, I had a terrible dream. In that horror, I was at home in the company of friends having a meal. Then something strange happened. A glass filled with passion-fruit juice located nearest to my side, splintered into smithereens. The pieces scattered in all directions about the feet of the four of us seated around the transparent, glass, makeshift dining table. That piece of furniture, the height of a footrest, was used in real life to entertain domino guests in my humble Elliston Flats residence in working-class, parochial Kingston.

We were all spared the liquid, and nobody suffered any injuries. I rose from my chair to pick up the particles, but they became invisible, and I fought to stay conscious before stumbling out of my slumber.

It was about four in the morning, as I lay awake, thinking about some ominous connection that might have had something to do with the meaning of the nightmare. The familiar sound of a multitalented nightingale disrupted my contemplation, as the multicolored midget mocker flaunted a few keynotes to exercise her vocal cords in that early-bird rehearsal. Meanwhile, her melodiously unfading voice serenaded my neighbors' last-minute beauty sleep to cut it short for the ordinary workers, who were soon to get busy boarding daybreak buses.

The long-tailed songbird was sitting only God knows where, giving out its timely chant, as if to alert its superiors that their time to start the ball rolling had drawn nigh. Wherever she perched, a sleeper would most definitely wonder whether she possessed a timepiece, to be so accurately punctual with her wakeup call that matched every single day she entertained her audience.

It just seemed to happen during those incredible moments when a responsible citizen was half-asleep, but could subconsciously tell when the engine of some city shuttle, was about to throttle on the spot for a good few minutes. That was after the mass-transit conveyor cleared the steep corner of the incline overlooking the sprawling community of Elliston Flats townhouses below.

From known routines, my stream of consciousness pictured the first automobile screeching its brakes to a stop, on its way down to August Town. While the engine idled, the carrier relieved itself of its yawning passengers, who had the look of Friday fans and bed-huggers. Those waiting to ascend peered impatiently inside, while the standing capacity crowd inched its way towards the lone exit. Meanwhile, the seated riders displayed their readiness with their bags in hand. Still, others raised themselves in place to a semi-standing position, leaning their heads to avoid the overhead compartment, while they clutched at the back of their sitting space. A few bided their time to slip into the crawling cue at the slightest opening.

Later that morning, as the sun peeped from behind Long Mountain, I gave the dream a more serious thought, and fancied that I had to be at my best behavior for the days ahead. It was just as uncanny as it was uncomfortably difficult to explain. And so, I decided not to share it even with the folks, who found themselves in this mind-trapping intoxication, perhaps by some twist of the gods' good-humored imagination.

I knew that I had planned to retry the American embassy, since it was one year to the date that I was turned down on my last trip. That strike was actually the second such attempt, given that on the first, I stuck to the truth and nothing but the truth, yet paid dearly for such sobering shortsightedness. For the more recent punt, I dressed up my cause a little more, to guard against rejection for not having enough ties, like I was told in a letter on that heart-piercing occasion. But again, I came up empty.

In my estimation, that repulsion felt like a bitter pill to swallow, no buts about that. And anyone who rejoined the yearly line to muscle up for another grueling grill, like a Hilary Clinton put on the spot to speak for her sanction of the war in Iraq, would agree that it was the worst failure on the face of the earth, never mind in Jamaica. I learned from my mistakes, hence this third tour of the embassy's lobby promised to pay greater dividends.

In those days, Oxford Road, home to the superpower's visa-overseers, experienced lines that snaked standstills, flushing debutantes and deviants onto Knutsford Boulevard - the good, bad and the ugly - all taking a shot at pulling off the precious commodity. A man had nothing to lose except sleep and sweat, waiting a dozen months to place his stake. Of course, that was contingent on whether his charms or prayers paid off, after nervously speaking through a microphone to make his case.

"I hope it's the man I face this time," said one woman, whose temporary bed consisted of cardboard boxes to meet the standing occasion. Like a buyer on *Black Friday** in the USA, she had spent the whole night in the parking lot across from the two-story, security-tight building that was the source of disappointment for many casualties. Those victims all sacrificed sleep just to be counted in the quota, when the names were called. There were two females and one male at the window. "I have no luck with women," the same contender continued, showing signs of incertitude and hope in equal and contradictory proportions.

The haggard man, with whom she communicated her innermost feelings, had some concerns and misgivings of his own. He had already paid the hustlers, who like the applicants, remained on their toes tending to the visa spin-offs. These parasites collected sizeable sums from filling out forms for illiterate aspirants, or from snapping photos for country bumpkins, who were too timid to find their way around, even too tired to think straight about emigration matters.

I had already made up my mind that I was going to be in the galloping on April 10, 1994 and that was sealed and signed with my staying power. The very morning before I took my sentimental journey, I woke up to hear a honeybee buzzing inside my master bedroom, where I had retired earlier the pertinent night. Being too immersed in my early-dawn doze, I ignored the intruding insect that dillydallied above the glass louvers. It basked in the light of the sixty-watt bulb above it, while I rolled over and continued the snooze.

Then tragedy struck, and a sting to my right side had me springing out of bed like I was shot from a cannon. At first, I didn't know what got me on the hip to get me on my feet. But then my intuition kicked in as a reminder of the nagging sounds that the nectar-sucking fly had transmitted in seeking an escape route; the exact distress signal that got my divided attention an hour or so before.

The pain was excruciating, what with the thorn digging its way deeper in my side, as an indicator that the suicidal organism had only just released its venom. However, I suddenly developed a kind of appreciation for the discomfort that tugged at my forbearance, indicating that this was a contact of contrary. Somehow, something good would come out of my seeming misfortune. My mind flashed impetuously in the direction of the US Embassy, and a positive attitude overcame my aplomb. The interview couldn't come quick enough.

"So Mr. Welds, why do you want to visit the US?" asked Barry.

His nameplate gave away his identity. He was the male of the three interrogators, for whom the woman expressed preference, while they perhaps inadvertently drove fear in the hearts of the waiting crowd. And I just happened to endure the unappealing disincentive, when I overheard the murmuring woman on that same day I dropped in to make my appointment.

He seemed well rested and relaxed, so much the better. My assignment to him was made possible by sheer shifting my buttocks along some chairs, arranged to form a quadrangle in the waiting area. The sliding motion from one seat to the next, guaranteed that each candidate got one of the three consulates, depending on which microphone was vacant. Everything worked in my favor, and Barry was a blessing delivered to me on a platter.

I thought of the woman who morbidly feared facing the female interviewers. I could allow the memory of her to bewitch my efforts with the negativity that she released in the universe. Or, I could empower my move with the positive thought that whoever appeared in front of me, would paradoxically come under my spell, even for the ten or fifteen minutes that I was expected to spend under that officer's inspection. I chose the latter as my propeller to get Barry to see something in me that deserved a second consideration.

It was about eleven o'clock when the day's visa seekers sat listlessly in the line, not knowing what to expect based on past experience. Like saints outside the pearly gate, awaiting hot tickets to heaven, occupants shuffled across their seats, making for the end, in readiness to approach one of the three windows equipped with the speaking apparatuses.

It seemed most of the earlier entrants were turned back, judging from the white sheet of paper that each reject was given with the bad news. Apparently, those who found favor to be among the chosen few, were told to submit their passports while they walked away empty-handed, sporting the unenviable tact of some reversed psychology. There was an aura of timidity within the service area, and only the cracking voices of respondents, quaking at the commanding intonation of the interviewers, could be heard in direct correspondence. My vociferous projection was about to change that tempo, however.

"I plan to do further studies, and I want to seek out a college in what better place than the US of A!" I said, searching to find the nitty-gritty, which could put me one step ahead of a man, I imagined to be versed in the business of intelligence and its fields.

I was really an ardent believer in the power of knowledge, but to say that I had an immediate academic motive for leaving my country, was nothing but a white lie. However, I inferred that a fellow, like the one staring deep in my soul to find the faintest fault, would be definitely impressed by any semblance of my scholastic interest.

Barry was a Caucasian character, and although the separating wall of glass jutted upwards from a counter-high threshold, I could envisage that he was of a stocky build and medium height. He spoke as if he knew me from somewhere, and his warm smile gave me the confidence that I had a consulate on my side. I almost took his pleasant personality for granted, not anticipating that his next questions were carefully orchestrated.

"What do you plan to study?" asked the beaming Barry, fixing his stare with paramount penetration. I knew that I had to display spontaneity to corroborate the authenticity of my story. And as if by divine intervention, I managed to do just that rather convincingly.

"I was reading for my Master of Science in Public Administration, but due to the death of my father, I had to abort the program. Now, I think it's time to get on with my life," I said, like I was selling myself on a billion dollar contract, prepared to even gain some mileage from the loss I actually experienced a few years before. There was nothing undignified about this alibi. If anything, it was the speed at which it was able to come to my rescue and defense that made it rather astounding.

Perhaps it was my dad's spirit that spoke from the grave on my behalf to make my venture smooth sailing. And not surprisingly so, because years before his departure, he had browbeaten that I gave my place of birth a break, and cast my net in more 'productive' places. Henri, as he was affectionately known, was a man of little willpower, but the little he had, he hoped would go a long way in making pacesetters out of the three sons he brought into the world, to complement their three sisters.

He never lived long enough to see me obeying his commandment, but he could have been my guarding angel putting words in my mouth, and the right ones at that. Like a monkey swinging from branch to branch, Barry browsed my abilities to find my breaking point. However, I stayed with him wherever he went, like kids playing hide and seek in any event. And between each stop, his two forefingers flipped through my travel document with the slight force of a mere formality. It was as if he started on the premise that I had the stamp already, and I was the only person who could stand in my own way. That was a stark difference from former times when I started with a deficit, and played the catch-up match, filling in the blanks with points from each answer to get up to scratch.

"Mr. Welds, I notice the space at fifteen is empty. Any particularly reason or explanation?"

It was indeed the question that addressed my cash value, and that in and of itself was a ticklish affair. But boy, was I broke! The worst of any applicant's woes was to show how much he was worth, using bank statements, and money my part of the world was as scarce as an open secret. However, once people knew they were about to go for the big one, they made sure that they were not deficient in that department, even if they had to beg, borrow or steal.

And so, some people padded their power in local banks, by inveigling friends and relatives to transfer hefty figures to inflate the balances of those chasers, in time for these appointments. The downside was that many risk-takers ran into diverse difficulties, resulting in regular post-cover-up squabbles. Money, being the magnet for mischance and misappropriation, tempted many to be mean in not returning what never belonged to them in the first instance.

Meanwhile, the mad rush to leave Jamaica since the 1980s put the consulates on high alert, and often many seekers were tarred with the same brush of insincerity. That never stopped thousands from trying just about anything to get by the ogres. And according to a female friend of mine, she was so frustrated when, despite her preparedness in 'financial assets', she was denied the stamp once again.

As Brenda related from experience, based on being turned down over the years, she thought she understood just what the iron-fisted fellows ordered. She managed to secure all the requirements and then some, except the sagacity that she should tailor her attitude to fit the unforgivable fact of the matter. Instead of allowing good sense to avail by waiting on instructions, Brenda approached the chute with that by-hook-or-by-crook, *now-what* look. Then she pushed everything in hand inside the acceptor, quickly arousing suspicion on the other side of the counter.

The officer did not hesitate to send her back to the beginning, perhaps indirectly telling her to wipe that frown from off her face. She never stated the gender, but any male or female consulate was capable of showing who decided the destiny of people like Brenda, in visa ventures. Hence, she left thinking that nobody knew how to please the chiefs, even when money was never an issue.

On my part, experience also taught wisdom through the devil's pyramid. And so I kept it real, displaying the most imperturbable perseverance and composure imaginable. I hadn't declared any figures, but I knew I was on top of my game. I had come across as genuine from the start of my interview, and I just figured I had to keep it that way in an unconquerable show of consistency.

"I don't believe in banking," I declared opportunely, making a sound statement that suited the economic climate at the time.

Banking had gone to the dogs, and many lost thousands in different institutions due to insolvency. Nobody knew when another money giant would collapse, claiming to fall on hard times. Like I said, in the past, some closed their doors in the faces of desperate costumers, leaving the losers to weep.

Consequently, I had not said anything that any well-thinking coordinator, living in some undisclosed section of the volatile country, couldn't understand about someone in my position. However, it was a rational thing to say that I didn't have the necessary confidence in bogus banking. But it would have been totally unacceptable not to be able to come up with an alternative source of saving.

"So how do you save?" Barry probed.

The questions began to become staccato, sensitizing the intensity to indicate that the crunch had been heightened. Admittedly, saving was a crucial statement of stability, and I couldn't leave this aspect of my character unsaid, without losing points on my credibility chart. My economic ties had to be consolidated, and this fine-tuning question had the potential of biting out a chunk of my chances to keep that invisible emblem of assurance in place.

"Animals are bigger deals," I asserted, with a kind of recommending slant to prove my interest.

"Where do you keep them, certainly not in the capital?"

"My parents have enough arable land in the east. You're welcome to see my handwork on your day-off," I extended an invitation to Barry auspiciously.

What a lie! In St. Thomas where my immediate family originated, land was no problem, so he got that part right. However, predial thieves worked round the clock, rounding up beasts to make a living, and animal husbandry was the farthest thing from a farmer's mind. Worst of all, people in that parish had little to be thankful for, living in desperation, where the ordinary folks fought hard to find their dinner. Hence, nobody had shots to waste on polecats.

But I must have falsified my above response tantalizingly to appeal to Barry's passion, so much so that he repaid with a wide smile of endorsement. One good thing about Americans was that animals were a priority, and anyone who could prove that herding different breeds was his forte, would definitely secure a ticket to the next show. I felt lucky to be in the right place, to use the right trick, to pull the wool over the eyes of my man on this occasion.

"What kind of animals do you raise?"

This was not a tough question, yet it found me completely unprepared. I couldn't blame Barry for my lapse of judgment, in not expecting such a relevant question to match my last reply. On the contrary, he was simply manifesting what had certainly become his keen interest in my animal instincts. In other words, he had explicitly demonstrated a very attentive disposition to the point of surrealism, and therefore, I trusted that he was not out to stump me. By then, it was evident that he bought my story hook, line and sinker.

If I fumbled to find the names of some simple animals to continue the trend of thought, I would have buried myself under a pile of stones, and would have perhaps deserved to stay there. Hence, I opened my mouth, hoping something befitting would fall out, to fall into place with everything I already stated. There were many choices, but two managed to engage my lips in a verbal symphony.

"Cows and goats," I said, trying to keep a straight face.

Sometimes a man had something lying dormant inside of him, but never knew it until the situation presented itself. For, I always felt that mastering the art of fabrication was never going to be my strong point. I had tried it before, but midway the façade, I froze like a choked comedian, who suddenly realized he didn't belong to the stage.

In my case, a good detective could read my eyes and facial expressions to know that I was like a geek on his first date. However, with my dream hanging in the balance, I must have been capable of convincing even a high court judge, against compelling evidence to make my wish become his command. Barry skimmed a final page in my book before pronouncing his judgment.

"Okay Mr. Welds, pick up your visa on the thirteenth," he instructed, while putting my particulars where the luck of the draw had its collection.

I wanted to scream, laugh and jump all at the same time. I had a strange sensation, losing control of the magnetic field of free-flowing emotions that flooded every nerve in my mortal body. A voice inside my head told me to put all my efforts in one basket to keep some sobriety. It reminded me that I just got off the hook with a lie, and the gullible guy who made the escape possible, was still within eyeshot.

Barry was finished with me and I didn't even know what to do next, whether I should stand and stare at his masculine face, or walk off for everyone to notice that I was stepping like a cat cantering on hot bricks. When I finally did something, I got everything confused - window, exit, walkway between the chairs - all seemed to have new meanings. I collided with a glass door on my way out, as I tried to get away from the building before Barry changed his mind.

The couple days it took to retrieve my passport, enriched with my travel license to the mainland, felt like I had sweated out a month. My mind radiated in every direction.

"What if Barry wavered? Will he research the information that I gave him?" I tortured myself, thinking deeply that anything could still go wrong to end the enormity of my celebration.

It suddenly occurred to me that success was something with a strategic twist, requiring utmost maturity. I learnt that after its achievement, it was a test of mental strength to stay focused in a positive mode for any extended period of time, if all one knew about was hardship all his life. I felt like I understood why lottery winners were usually overcome by stupidity to go broke in no time. Therefore, I decided not to let even the breeze in on the secret of my acquisition, until after I collected my prize on the day designated.

April 13, 1994 was easily the best day of my life. The night before, I suffered a bout of insomnia being too excited and anxious, and I just couldn't sleep for more than fifteen minutes a wink. The morning started with the nightingale as usual, while the community slowly wriggled to its feet, according to the day's activities. The sun set up its show of radiance, using rays to twinkle the dews on the green grass, that reminded everyone using the spiraling, hilly roadway in front of 10 Golden Avenue, that Spring was already on its way.

The weather on that side had no other way of indicating that there was a break in its bearing, apart from compensating with a little precipitation, worthy of making some peasants wake up to witness it. The beauty that encased the picturesque setting of that Wednesday, told me that I was all set to take my place in the sun.

When I left Oxford Road that afternoon, to ford the lunchtime traffic that crawled to a ten-minute stop every so often, something assured me more than ever that everything was going great. After surveying the whole Jamaican scenery, I thought of just burning all my bridges, since as far as I was concerned, the ship was already sinking. Besides, when I looked far away, I imagined that the land of the free, not to mention the home of the brave, was already celebrating my arrival!

* *The Friday after Thanksgiving when stores countrywide sold items on sale, at which time customers slept in line to get the limited goods on a first come first served basis.*

CHAPTER TWO

Long Road Winding Turns

"The road to hell is still paved with gold," I reminded myself, hoping that those words I heard when I used to be a staunch Christian, were a figment of my religious imagination. "This is a golden opportunity and nothing, absolutely nothing is going to rain on my parade, *God Bless America*." Somehow, there was a stigma at the back of my mind, telling me that the picture often painted of *The Big Apple*, for instance, sounded too good to be true.

Still, I fought back mentally to stay positive, thinking that, like Daniel's horny dream in *The Holy Bible* signified some seemingly endless voyage with a light at the end of the tunnel, my adventure was perhaps hopefully one of a bad beginning that was poised to make a good ending. But never in my wildest dream did I believe that I would find myself walking on the sidewalk of an infernal odyssey, until the day I decided to make the American dream my reality.

"Nothing good comes easy, remember?" I consoled myself, so that I didn't become a deterrent to my own destiny. I drew my own conclusions, and stood to be corrected by the events that rocked my world, while I continued to dream.

My visa was either a blessing or a curse in disguise, and I was about to find that out one way or another. Blessing in the sense that, if what I heard and saw on television was true, then I might soon be wallowing in the lap of luxury. Curse, if after all that was said and done, by the time I got there, the pie in the sky was already taken, and my slice was indeed gone with the wind.

"But there's enough in this life to go around for everyone. You'll get your share!" I was too torn between two ideas.

As a matter of fact, what was about to unfold throughout the visa aftershocks of my life, could redefine the term, 'American dream', to the point where mine must have begun the moment I got that stamp of approval. In actuality, it was one thing to learn about other parts of the globe, going by what others said, or by reading some book to get up to speed with lifestyles, or even letting it come to me electronically in the comfort of my own home. But there was absolutely no way anybody could put it across as accurately as the experience of getting it first-hand.

Time flew after I got the go-ahead, and I calmed down a little when my options opened to secure a teaching job in the British Virgin Islands. There, my salary was quoted on delivery in US dollars.

"The greens? Well, look no further!" That was pretty easy to think and to say, like a one-shot boxer who went down early in a title fight, knowing he could live on the runner-up reward.

The ambience in the archipelago of eastern Caribbean rocks was simply irresistible. Anegada, which meant 'drowned land' according to the Spanish, was a spectacle to souvenir. Virgin Gorda, labeled by those conquistadors because of its shape, had humungous boulders to hide a generation. Tortola, with Road Town as its capital, attracted the best boaters from around the globe. Regular regatta made the hilly, ferry-driven resort the next likely hideout for which many vacationers would vouch, once they had been there and done that.

If peace of mind were a thing that money could buy, these islands would easily be the richest places on earth. Yet three-quarters of a decade later, I landed in San Juan en route to *La Gran Manzana*, to see what I had been missing since I got the green light. I perhaps would have made myself at home in these safe haven islands, weren't it for the craze and fever that I had caught from the students and inhabitants in those places.

I made some good friends there, Pat included, and it was people like this pregnant mistress, who made me feel as though I walked on my ambitions. Two weeks before taking her fetus to full term, she went missing, and in those small communities where if an athlete ran too hard he ended up in the ocean, it was not hard to tell that the two thousand close-knitted, gossip-loving Virgin Gordans dwindled by one.

No news was good news, and I knew her absence couldn't have been anything beyond the norm, since incidents, great and small, were delivered right at everyone's doorstep with the speed of lightning by two-footed ambulances.

"Long time no see," I said, taking advantage of the local lingo, to do as the Romans did while I was stationed in Rome.

Pat had lost her pouch and she seemed to have gotten a spring in her steps in direct exchange. Perhaps it was because she had a successful labor, but I thought it was best getting it straight from her mouth, once she was not at a loss for speech.

"I went to have my baby in St. Thomas. All my relatives are US citizens," she bragged, suggesting her newborn wouldn't have settled for anything less.

How could that happen when the British Virgin Islanders were supposed to be, as their title implied, the dependents of their motherland? There was a little bit of history lesson for my silly-Billy brain, and Pat was just the one to become my teacher in time.

Firstly, these miniature islands used the US currency instead of the pounds, and according to what the predecessors passed down the line, it dated back to those fishing days when both the British and United States territories conducted business, and decided their own terms of trade. Secondly, they were fully Americanized from birth, capitalizing on the proximity of the borders, and that had become inbred for successive generations.

Every compass located St. Thomas, not to be confused with the parish that I lied about in my brush with Barry, years before knowing that this namesake even existed as part of the universe. It was one of three pieces of land that the USA paid Denmark twenty-five thousand dollars to leave alone, generations before - St. Croix and the diminutive St. John completing the misappropriation.

The three were the strongest links in the chain, strengthening the rest of the resorts. Island hoppers, who went in search of better living standards, quickly became the Christopher Columbus of the century, making these spoonfuls of sandy soil pieces of paradise to be exploited. Movie stars had been known to pitch permanent tents for retreating purposes, investing in a few of the million little pieces that comprised these eastern Caribbean cul-de-sacs.

On any given day, Tortolans and their neighbors gaffed on verandas to watch ferries ride roaring waves, decks brimming with the young and old, as the vessels negotiated chartered grounds, with hulls bobbing and weaving to the rhythms of dancing, blue waters. Those with upper quarters under the weight of tourists could be seen tilted and tossed about like toys, pushed by swells that plunged the unbalanced boats to near submersion. Then the sea cruisers buoyantly bounced back upwards to the sigh and relief of many passengers, who feared dark seas.

There were incidents when cowards died a thousand times before reaching their destination. Times when their hearts sailed through their lips, to cause the perplexed people to search beneath their seats for life-saving jackets that waned from inactivity. At other times, the shuttle steamers plied through thick clouds of dust, which coated the atmosphere in the aftermath of the rabid anger that the fully awakened volcano in Montserrat, rained down on the region.

The wind this side of the West Indies always seemed angry too, as if working over and above the call of duty to create a wider space between landforms. Air whistled in the azure above life-claiming waters, while long-billed seagulls braved the deep to charge at the tides, as their wings flopped powerfully to show that they were numb to the dangers in sight.

Many of these birds of prey with similar intention, hovered in an aerial hopscotch to take turns, nose-diving and clutching their catches between razor-like, pointed beaks, as the large snappers and the like, wriggled while sliding down the voracious gullets of the gulls. In the distance, those same parasitic flocks laughed at fishermen in canoes resembling paper copies from an overhead view, mocking the contenders as the stalkers risked their lives, to try their hands at getting even one successful haul for a day.

Understandably, the ferrying along with the back and forth fanfare, caught the attention of the wrong crowd, and if nobody expected illicit activity to fester, that would have been optimism at its optimum. Even those with accents common to other places, found a way to show proof that they were born in this few square-feet of land, that must have been overpopulated on paper overnight. Birth papers sold like hot cakes, when those from far and wide realized that that was all it took to travel interstate.

Pablo was a Jamaican I met on a BWIA flight when I was coming back from my two-week vacation. A dark-haired, hairy-skinned six-footer, this dude had the look of being no pushover, and one who it would seriously take more than a couple scores of pegs and yards of barbwire to make his den. A very pensive party, or a man of few words, this brother's brain seemed to tick overtime, trying to figure out where to make the next move to land his feet. His bulbous eyes seemed accustomed to close during daytime to make way for nightlife, or some kind of nocturnal excitement. He bopped in his strut like a hustler or a hardened thug, who traveled only in the fast lane; one who never tinkered with anything that would take a lifetime to achieve. A slow town would have nothing to offer a fellow like Pablo, except boredom and frustration.

He and I were stranded in St. Maarten when our connecting flight floundered, and we got acquainted when we roomed in a hotel to continue the trip the following morning. Pablo apparently knew when to hold up, and the night went well with little to do, apart from taking a rest on two small beds, made convenient for occasions like the one we encountered.

We were from different parts of Jamaica, and we had contrasting work experiences and inclinations. I found out that underneath this tough-guy image, there was a good personality in the rough that was waiting to be polished. However, I was not so sure about the amount of time it would take for any meaningful progress to be made, should a Good Samaritan decide to give the task a try.

A cellular phone was a thing of the future, and there was no way of getting the message across to Pablo's pick-up at Tortola's only airport, hence the loss of signals. However, he had better luck than I did, on this journey to somewhere out of this world for any one Jamaican at a time. Perhaps that was why I showed compassion more than anything else. I remembered the agonizing wait I endured in a small room in which Emma, the on-duty immigration cop, tucked me to turn me back, at this cricket-pitch-airstrip port of disembarkation.

The air traffic in this enclave could only accommodate the like of LIAT, a single-engine carrier that wouldn't run off the one hundred meters of runway, to interfere with canoes and sailboats in the surroundings.

"Lou, wait!" shouted Emma, calling out to the pilot who had his foot on the pedal, about to lift clutch for the sky.

Yes, it was as informal as that, and the smaller the plane, the opportunity to see who was talking or sitting behind the wheel, was so much easier. The afternoon was slow, and except for the fifteen or so passengers that had arrived earlier, workers were just fiddling with their nails, waiting for some other short, snappy flight to buzz in like an annoying housefly. Then when the pilot did his part, if he were fortunate, he might have a few outgoing, listless loners to accompany him on his way back. If not, he was really not scheduled to wait on time to take his course through the air.

Emma was simply telling Lou that he had company in case he didn't know, and that person incidentally was no stranger to controversy.

"I can't speak for anybody else," the chocolaty, buxom woman of about thirty years declared, "but I am not letting you through," she emphasized, simultaneously stroking her chest, to show she was dead serious with her take on that final conclusion. I couldn't totally blame her for being so strict, since it was my fault not to have remembered the name and address of my host, when it was clearly given to me by a good buddy of mine.

I didn't know why she made it sound optional, because there was nobody else in sight to override her decision. Then it suddenly struck me that I could use my manly tease to bring her to her knees.

"So you mean a beautiful woman like you would be only too willing to get rid of a jaunty gentleman like me?" And I looked her in the eyes to induce the ultimate attraction. Meanwhile, I saw her emotions coming out, and the tigress in her dissipating.

"You look like somebody I know," she softened up, as I slowly overpowered her with my charms. "Welds? I know a guy by that name living in East

End. Is he your blood?" I suddenly became that familiar face, while she was faced with reversing that harsh stance that she took to send me away.

Within the next half an hour I had Emma eating out of my hands, and realizing that she seemed vulnerable at one point, I kind of acquiesced that I might be in fact related to my look-alike. She oscillated back to her senses a little, after she slackened the noose around my neck.

"I won't give you more than two weeks to find your keeper," she said. "If you don't, you can kiss these places goodbye." She stamped my passport like she was placing a kiss of life on it, and I walked away wondering whether Lou was left to enjoy his journey.

Two weeks was all I ever wanted to get a foot in the door, and to employ my power to attract people with my personality. I applied for a teaching position and was soon accepted at a school where Emma's separated husband taught Physical Education on Wednesdays. After a while, Emma and I became good friends, so that I had my own way with just about anything, including getting her to address Pablo and his personal dilemma.

I used my clout to clear the first-timer at customs in Tortola, and though we went our separate ways, we found a way to stay in touch.

Hardly had he been around for two days, when Pablo focused his binoculars on New York, courtesy of a birth-paper bargain he struck with a St. Thomas link. And I was the first to be informed of the plan he was pedaling.

"I have to come up with the thousand dollars," he said, trying to persuade me to lend him the amount until he made it to *The Big Apple*. "It's the real shit. I know somebody who got through just like that," he continued, hell-bent on collecting some funds out of my hands.

"I don't see that kind of money," I pretended to be sailing in the same boat of desperation, by referring to my mortgage obligations back home.

I really didn't support him leaving because although we lived in two separate islands, we spoke everyday, and we had somehow bonded like two pilgrims in strange lands. I learned a lot too, that traveling leveled the playfield to sometimes invite loneliness. Now, that had the power of a pulley wheel to break just about anyone, even someone who thought he was *all that*. And that individual could be driven to welcome those of dissimilar interests to his company, like the prodigal son who ate with pigs, during hard times.

But Pablo had an obsession with a young woman, who had migrated to the USA five years before. She was grounded in the city that never slept, waiting for her immigration papers to realize *her* dreams. While the grass was greener and growing, the horse was already starving in its stable, and Pablo considered his newfound contrivance a wonderful opportunity to regroup with his girlfriend. That would have been regardless of whether she was somewhere entangled in some marriage-for-convenience mess, waiting for some crack-head to cut her loose with a divorce. Whatever! He was prepared to cross the desert like an Arab man, though he knew it was going to cost him one grand - and more.

This crazy risk-taker decided not to part with the idea, and each time we spoke, he moaned and groaned about the money. I figured he was looking toward me as his savior in the situation, so I screened my calls. And for over a month, we gave each other a break.

Then one day, someone called me long-distance, and it turned out to be Pablo half a world away, telling me about his mixed fortune. Everything worked as planned, except that the woman he went after, had become a totally different monster when he eventually saw her, and he needed psychiatric intervention to get his head back where it belonged.

I didn't have to go along Pablo's route to get to the north, thanks to Barry and my ingenuity. But San Juan International Airport became my gateway on May 27, 2001. The Puerto Rican capital parched in the typical Caribbean heat, while opportunistic hustlers hovered behind the prohibiting lines, surrounding the nucleus of traveling population and authorities. The green vegetation, visible in the rolling plains, testified that the often eighty-degree temperatures had no devastating effects on plant life, as long as the cool complementary breeze got in to give a balance of nature.

The deafening sounds of landings and take-offs had a gripping guise that induced the fear factor in anyone with a phobia for flying. That aura emitted a kind of chilling reminder to whisper a word of prayer, just in case something went wrong. Meanwhile, the arrival area was filled with curious faces, some waiting anxiously to see if the next person to exit the tinted, view-from-inside-out glass-door would be the one to be collected. Placard-bearing taxi-operators stood by to display names, each on which, they hoped they would soon be in a position to put a face. American Airline check-in counter was located a good walk down, past this section, and I had to drag my two suitcases plus a shoulder-strap bag, after getting off the elevator on the third floor.

I was young and athletic, hence perhaps that wouldn't have bothered me so much, had I not been already faced with enough frustration for one day. But my distress had gotten off to a blistering start, when a string of disappointments created a chain reaction. I had made an arrangement for a taxi to take me to town, but after waiting till the appointed time, the negligent driver failed to honor his agreement. That was how I ended up on a public bus, bound for the busy terminal.

I became anxious that I would miss my 2:30 flight, since I was already biting into my 1:30 check-in itinerary. In my rush, I must have taken leave of my senses, not to have asked the chauffer whether he was going straight to *Departure*, and consequently, I took my stop a little too previous.

The thoroughfare thereof was as busy as the *I-95*, but I needed to beat it across two winding turns before getting on to the airport property. Taxis zoomed by my ears, before I could even make out the make, model, or even the color of the carriages. Meanwhile, like a horse-drawn chariot, I struggled with two hamper-like containers, packed to capacity with my necessaries that were supposed to start me off in the mainland. Sweat poured down my spine like I had taken a dip in the Hudson River. And as for the tributaries on my face, I felt like I needed a third hand to wipe away the salty liquid that burned my eyes as though it contained chlorine.

Subjected to that inconvenience, I skipped to make it between merciless vehicular traffic that honked at my seeming carelessness. By the time I scurried safely to the other side, I had to take a breather, feet flanked by the luggage while I stood, totally forgetting that I was pressed for time.

So I got to the third floor, when perhaps a remaining half of the scheduled patrons took turns to get their belongings onto those busy conveyor belts. Such a big difference from what I knew, based on my unlimited track record in flying. Everyone was weighing in, before being marshaled off to a chute-like projection connected to the entrance of the throttling aircraft, no steps necessary.

I was the only one of African, more so Jamaican descent, standing in the file behind blond-haired and blue-eyed people with strange accents, belonging to far-away places like even Australia. They looked like seasoned campaigners, who had been in iron-birds so many times, that perhaps a crash was the only thing that they had ever cheated in the air. The attendants, I imagined, were Spanish, and they had a good thing going with these said strangers in terms of interaction, based on the facial expressions and reciprocal laughter from both ends.

Then I stepped up to one smartly attired official, and greeted him with a smile. After that, I released my documents inside the cubbyhole, and those included my notable, blue passport that was as big as a textbook. Miguel was his name and he couldn't have been more than in his late twenties, judging from his youthful voice and wrinkle-less forehead. His countenance changed for the worse when I took up my position, even before he took charge of my travel paraphernalia.

"So what are you going to the US for now?" he asked, as if he were speaking to someone on the *Top Ten Most-Wanted List.*

Miguel looked me up and down, with the seriousness of a magistrate of the nineteen sixties. Apparently he might have been anxious to get this one out of the way, with little or no concerns about any damage caused. With a scrutiny like his, I felt like I had escaped from a cage, and any second, I was supposed to hear some alert system go off to incite my recapture and return to seclusion. I was put on the spot to give a good account of myself, and my self-esteem extraordinaire kicked in high gear. I had no problem spotting the reason for the tension, before I rose to the occasion, keeping calm under the existing underestimation.

"I am going the USA to seek out a college because I intend studying there," I said, slowly selecting my words to break the pace of the careless service representative. I could sense that at the sound of academics, he began to loosen his grip on my character. Nobody, including Miguel, could overpower the edge of education, and that fact always saved my day, whenever I became a victim under very precarious pressure, from those who often abuse their authority.

He began to rummage through my book very methodically as if to be assessing details. Which supposedly by then, he realized that that was the sensible thing to do in front of a man, who was proving to be a cut or two above the intelligence level usually required by a front desk clerk. I could tell that Miguel never went past his GED*, from observing his demeanor toward the public, his elementary vocabulary and his approach in expediting his responsibility. A teacher of umpteen years wouldn't have had any doubt in doing that spot-check evaluation of this novice, especially after having stood in a queue with eyes fixed on the little guy's inept coordination, and later being brought to bear the brunt of his obvious ignorance.

I somewhat knew what to expect, remembering Barry's bonus question, and I braced myself when Miguel finally came up for air to grill me again, though a little more tolerable this time.

"What do you plan to study?" It was like I was being re-interviewed with the stringency of an Oxford Road strategy, perhaps because the question and answer session mainly reminded me of a broken record. Well it wasn't broken, so why fix it? It worked for me then, so I didn't see why it shouldn't do the trick now. I hated repeating myself, especially when a lie was involved, but I thought that saying the same thing twice could only help rather than hinder at that point.

"I was doing an M Sc in Public Administration at the University of The West Indies in Mona, but for personal reasons I had to drop out. I plan to take up where I left off," I said, trying my best to be modest, to give this fellow a course in humility, while it still seemed workable.

Miguel started combing my passport again, with instant tranquility that suggested he was willing to give respect where it was deserved. Hopefully, he had learnt his lesson, not to judge a book by its cover, or better yet, its color. For, as far as I had observed, he never seemed to have known jack about the other folks who went ahead of me in the line, but that didn't affect his courtesy towards them. I wished I could rub it in a little more, and for that reason, an idea came to mind.

I knew I was in Puerto Rico, where Spanish was the first language of communication, and Miguel was bilingual for that matter.

"Va a ser mi primera vista de los Estados Unidos, y no tengo la menor idea de qué esperar!" I remarked, anticipating that such a switch would most definitely get *Papi*'s attention.

And it did, again confirming my suspicion that his inexperience was moving in tandem with his limited intelligence. I could see a million and one trifling issues pricking at his small mind, as he jumped from perusing the pages in my passport, to an intentional stare in my eyes. He appeared to struggle with convincing himself that nobody had switched places with me while he wasn't looking. As he blushed, I read his thoughts and these were the words that baffled his brain in bold letters: 'black, Jamaican, Spanish - never before seen in the same sentence!'

"Qué quieres esperar? La primera vez existe para todo y entonces no te preocupes," replied Miguel, slowly emerging from his stupor. I worked out that he was working his way with that response to test my depth with the language, and I was more than ready to match wits with the young stranger.

We went off tangent in a conversation that strayed way beyond traveling and migratory matters, totally forgetting the linear build-up behind my back. Meanwhile, curious white faces looked on, trying to reconcile a black man with a Jamaican accent, speaking Spanish as if it were his native talent.

We finally came to our senses that, though the amicable clash was an unfamiliar sight, it was just another day in the office. And although the spectacle caught the interest of the patient travelers, like a Venus Williams versus Justine Hennin *US Open* semi-final, people didn't have all day to get on with their business.

" Que tenga una inolvidable visita!" Miguel finally wished, almost inadvertently stamping the six-month time-limit on his two forefingers between the margins, instead of on the intended page. He was obviously too busy and generous, giving me the same kind of civility he gave to people of other nationalities - only that he delivered it to them for free, whereas I had to work hard for mine. That was perhaps one positive thing I elicited during that short space of time, hence I had to practice, just in case I might need the same skill for future refuge.

"Muchas gracias. Que disfrute el resto de tu trabajo," I replied, walking away with a cosmetic smile that disguised what was going on deep inside.

Once Miguel was out of sight, he was also out of mind, as I was old enough to know that many people were like animals in the wild. They sniffed strangers, and when they felt threatened by the presence of more productive people, their role was to pass the gold through fire, to satisfy their dirty hearts' desire.

I entered the aircraft after a doorway delay, caused by the attendant's inability to discern if the expiry date at the back of the passport was in fact March 2001 or 2007 - the last digit causing the stir. Connie, the stewardess, was just as cantankerous as Miguel (before he was compelled to take a second look), but I was too exhausted to set her straight. I simply waited for her to reappear, after she vanished with my book behind a curtain to confer with someone perhaps more sensible.

At last I took my seat in the five-row airbus, arranged with a television screen in each column. I also took a deep breath after I began to feel like Gulliver in the land of Lilliput. Having persisted through all the rigmaroles, I hadn't had much time to reflect on any plan of action, in the event that I was caught lying between a rock and a hard place.

The inside of the aircraft was a stark contrast to everything that occurred on the exterior. There were air-conditioned units hard at work to emit a low humming that pervaded the aisles. I sat next to the window, and peered down below to get a good view of underpaid laborers, scurrying to pack luggage of all descriptions in the belly of the carrier. I could tell that they were told to redouble their efforts, to see how much the airline could recover its reputation. In no time, the speeding trolleys disappeared to give the phenomenon its own space to reach for the sky. And we went up, up and away!

* *The standard USA high school level diploma*

CHAPTER THREE

Getting There

I was thousands of feet up in the air and little by little I was getting there - closer and closer to my American dream. But what was really *my* dream? I could not answer that question in so many words, but I knew that my own country had not proven itself capable of delivering the standard of living I deserved. America promised a lot more, and as far as I knew it, that piece of heaven on earth has been living up to its name even before I was born. Now, here I was, going to the land where many disappeared for years, only to return and build their dream house on a hill with oceanic view.

It was a five-hour trek, and apart from a few air pockets that jerked at my consciousness as a reminder that I was nowhere near land, the almost motionless aircraft, occasionally cutting through thick cirrus and cirrostratus clouds, soothed my mind. I uncontrollably drifted off, daydreaming about my childhood, when kids belonging to parents living in *The States*, were the young and privileged little kings and queens of our circles. That advantage drew envy and admiration from different angles.

Some kids just could not afford to ride the kinds of bicycles, or wear the sorts of shoes that came from *foreign*, provoking mixed reactions among young rivals. A lot of those taunting youths secured visas and *Green Cards* through the dual nationalities of their parents. The lucky bastards belittled those who barely knew how to ride a bus, not to mention ever saw an airplane on a runway.

My first day at Morant Bay High came immediately to mind during my trance-like contemplation. And Faith was the foremost figure that haunted my memory. She was this eagle-nosed, eleven-year-old, who had parents in *The States* to facilitate her lavished lifestyle. She must have created a first impression on the remaining forty-one of us in that class. The majority in the group met for the first time, with the exception of those who went to elementary school in the parish capital.

In those days, it was a privilege to gain one of the coveted spots, tenable at the only high school in St. Thomas. However, the primary academy in the center turned out the smartest and the greatest number of winners. Since an individual scholarship was the equalizer, it seemed there had to be a divider as the despiser. And some parents pushed for the prominence of their kids, putting up wealth to become sore providers.

Teachers were often moved by the affluence that some students exhibited, and even if the mentors didn't capitulate, there were always those kids who still flaunted what they had to see how far they could go with even the principal. Faith was one of these stalkers who tried to make up for her dumbness by showing off her experience in destinations.

"What did you do for the summer?" asked Miss Grant, our homeroom teacher to start us off on the right foot in our new environment.

A very understanding and compassionate lady who was fresh from teacher training, Miss Grant threw out a simple question that deserved a simple answer, to arouse interaction rather than jealousy. Then a slender little hand went up, and it belonged to Faith, who registered her interest to go first. One couldn't miss the beanpole kid, whose uniform on her body made her look more like a dressed up scarecrow.

"I went to New York," she bragged with an American accent, reminiscent of former times, when a goody-goody went to the urban center for merely three weeks, and came back tongue-twisting, as if she were originally from Paris.

Faith gave a simple enough answer, but certainly one that caused everybody to give her a second look, and she knew it. It was no secret that the average kid around there belonged to peasant parents, and most likely would deify somebody who had the world at the tip of her fingers.

This girl had gotten on her feet to make her statement, but after she realized how much attention it gave her, she refused to take her seat, turning her head with that Rudolph-the-red-nose-reindeer vindication. Her pride went before her fall, because we all lived to learn later that she was indeed one of the weakest links, and what she had done at the onset was her way of celebrating her fifteen minutes of fame.

Thereafter, she brought up the rear in every academic assessment, but to this day, there must have been a mental scar left on those who kept hearing about the biggest city in the world from as early as that age, without getting the opportunity to visit it. At least, foolish Faith did, and nobody could take that away from her.

The pilot broke my concentration with his announcement, using his incredibly inviting voice that perhaps put a television broadcaster to shame.

"Once again, American Airline is pleased to have you on board," the manly talker began, before reeling off a string of intelligible words, so comforting to those who flew. He had the knack to keep passengers pacified, and at the same time, he made some hearts pant languishingly to see the man behind the melody.

"What a coincidence!" I thought. "America is so great, that country can even find manpower to combine a brave pilot and fine announcer all in one," I considered, positively believing that I was heading for a place where I was going to be in good company. It was like all kinds of everything reminded me of America.

Thinking about manpower, my understanding of economics made me realize that USA ought to be the class act for everywhere else in the world. However, I also deduced that there had to be a downside to everything. And when droves of decent men ditched their patriotism for one place, something had to be at that epicenter to trigger that kind of attraction.

People sacrificed families, wives and children at a time to make life for themselves and those they left behind in some cases. Once again, I consulted my childhood memories to feed my animation, without taking stock of the seriousness of the unfathomable implications of the inspiring incidents. Nevertheless, I rambled on.

I went through my entire school life knowing Cliff without ever getting a good look at Kenny, his dad, who was always married to Myra, the mother of this traveling man's eight offspring. At that time, children were seen and not heard, but that didn't mean we weren't keen about things occurring around us, especially right under everybody's nose, in one little district called Mount Vernon.

The agrarian community, located in the western hills of St. Thomas, was more or less siphoned off by the Negro River that served the area, both as a source of farming and domestic accessories. The five thousand country folks in that vicinity could tell what each other cooked for dinner, and one regular meeting spot was in the riverbed on a Saturday. That was usually when Carlton, a bulldozer operator, detoured one hand of the seasonal stream, leaving shrimps, crawfish and eels at the mercies of the whole population.

People swarmed down like ants to pick up the flipping crustaceans and their cronies, and the long stretch of stones and gravels, came under intense pressure from the weight of trampling human feet. Along the rocky path, the backs of catchers crouched every now and then conceding to scrape up a major scoop, while the fish and things hopelessly put up a fight, in what was left of the trickling tide between the stones of various sizes.

Meanwhile, searchers put aside whatever metal containers they carried to channel all their energies, shifting larger rocks out of sockets, to bare creepy shellfish or slithering water snakes in hiding. Hands with buckets and bags made sudden jolts and jerks, to avoid the open claws that lunged at the trappers. Then later in the afternoon after the good time was over, and Carlton returned the river to its proper place, the seasoned smell of fishy foods rose to heaven, whisking its way through small windows that watched over each neighbor's backyard.

The best days to enjoy this kind of close-knitted activity came after a great big downpour, that lasted a week or two at one go. The rainy seasons paid us a visit in May and August, and a good saturation got people in the mood for all play and no work.

To start us off, the nearby Blue Mountains dressed up in full white, looking more like an avalanche of snow or Santa's beard, and we knew what was coming to act fast. Before long, the water was upon the whole village, causing everyone to lock away for the whole duration. The river overflowed its banks, reaching up to the dykes that were built years before to safeguard the enclave. At that point, people dared not take a chance to come in contact with the khaki-colored swells, that cascaded downstream with vengeance on minds of their own.

After a recession of the rain, two weeks later the water was as clear as crystal and ready to be cautiously approached. Nobody could go across but there were places along its course, where skinny-dipping suggested that happy days came around every now and then. The water was ripe and ready for early-morning and midday freshness, when children bathed and played in the sands, while mothers did the laundry, got hungry and made a big brushwood fire to cook.

While the boiling water in *Dutch pots* bubbled on, with fresh ground provisions dancing to the beat of the heat, the women stripped down to their underwear and splashed in the river, before settling down to a bellyful of the victuals. By the end of another week, the water populated thickly with various creatures, and cried out to fish-eaters for a helping hand to lighten the load. And history repeated itself, every time Negro River reached its pinnacle with flushes from that hill, known the world over for producing the aromatic *Blue Mountain Instant Coffee.*

Kenny missed out on this togetherness so that, to most of the younger generations, he was just another face in the crowd when he took his yearly trip to see his family. Strolling on the streets of that lowly locale, he stepped with his head high, like he was a *Megamillion* winner, strutting with that smoothness brought back from the USA, where he worked with sugarcane that might have sweetened his standoffishness.

When he was not clearing the trashy elongated crops in those snake-infested American estates, he was, I imagined, climbing apple trees to harvest the red or green fruits. At that time, I thought the apples were similar to the juicy pericarps that we used abundantly, as part of a fruitful diet in the eastern part of the island.

"But he could have stayed home to help raise the kids, if all he wanted was to work on sugar plantations! Mount Vernon was not short of that kind of busy running-around when it was crop time." I tried to reconcile the thought and action, plus the reality.

Then I remembered that it wasn't as easy as what I was conjuring. But, more like those Jamaican communities that produced the bulk of brown sugar, yet were also the largest recipients of the imported version of that very product. Half of the best part of St. Thomas landscape was under sugar production, and that provided staple employment for the surrounding areas. It went from clearing and planting in the base areas, to milling and grinding at the adjoining *Serge Island Sugar Estates*. The Pengelly's, multinational foreign investors of the day, conducted the whole works. This regimented rustic enterprise was stringent in the tropics, specifying cultivation and harvesting routines.

Men and women started the ball rolling, dressed directly to match what they did on any given day. In the fields, broad hats protected the participants from being pelted by the fury of the sun. Headmen abused the situation like everything else, propositioning wives of men, who were too busy chopping at juicy stalks in other parts far away. Tractors got in gear, dropping off tanks of water at accessible points, before swinging around, screaming their brakes to race back to their point of origins to repeat the process.

In the evenings, weary men wearing clothes stained with soot from 'slash-and-burn' sugarcanes, sang or whistled homecoming tunes. Meanwhile, they carried sharp bills or Spanish machetes over their shoulders, and marched on home to rejuvenate for the following day. And their lives were centered on their livelihood for as long as they needed money, and their only means of survival was still in their own hands.

Kenny was never honored as a king in his own country. He must have chosen to sell his worth abroad, being caught in that get-rich-quick frenzy. However, everything about him seemed rosy on the outside, up to the better part of the 1980s. People often wondered how Myra coped with her hubby's absence that she endured in silence, but it never took the meddlers too long to work out a working theory.

A woman had needs and Myra Phillips was no different. She knew very well how to slow down the aging clock, because as a full-time mother of so many, she didn't have a wrinkle to show. At the same time, she could still turn heads better than many of her juniors. This was one bird that never messed in her nest. She therefore kept her conduct beyond the borders, leaving the insiders to guess what she was cooking. That was always the case whenever she dressed up like a contestant in a beauty pageant, and headed for the front of the single cab serving the district.

Only a private investigator could perhaps get to the bottom of an affair she had with a cop of a higher rank. However, nobody had any picture to prove anything to Kenny, who might have had his own thing going on in his camp abroad. People showed little interest to denigrate her anyway, since Kenny's disappearance act had somehow given her the license to look out for herself.

The whole commitment with consent started somewhere in the 1950s. It was from then Kenny's trips home had strange meanings, and his children were all born behind his back after he left Myra knocked up on her own. Both he and Myra bore good fruits, and the community exercised discretion considering the inconvenience the couple underwent, but equally consigning some understanding that it was worth it.

However, in 1990 when the breadwinner was about to say goodbye to years of juggling home and away, he had a massive heart attack and never recovered. The funeral expenses would have been too great for the family, if the body were to have flown back in one piece. Consequently, he was cremated and his ash sent home in a bottle, for the loved ones to handle at their disposal.

That familiar jinx reminded me of Victor, who was unmarried but had a son to feed, while programmed to pick apples in America too. What a fine gentleman he was! Always smiling, he brought sunshine to anyone who knew him.

During the time when music and entertainment had a larger version of the contemporary CD known as LP and 45, Victor used to bring back the best sound systems from the United States. My parents used to pay him for the peak Panasonic brand that he cleared at customs, under the pretext of personal use. And on a Sunday morning, the speakers pounded with religious rhythms in our home, while awakening jealousy and competition from around the neighborhood.

On a Friday or Saturday night, Al green, Marvin Gaye and The Drifters, to name a few, reached out and touched the hearts of everybody, regardless of age, with volumes that echoed in the distance. Who could forget Victor, the peaceful, soulful brother, who made his good manners and desirable demeanor do all the talking?

Sadly, all good things came to an end when a dangerous serpent silently spewed venoms into the veins of the soft-spoken fellow, as he reached for an apple covered with leaves. The vipers were always known to exist in those conditions, and many pickers, including the victim, knew the killers could strike at any moment.

When the elegiac news broke in Mount Vernon about Victor's untimely death, the Sunday dinner that the normal family put every effort into making, turned into water on everybody's table. The rice cooked with red peas and freshly squeezed coconut milk, chicken on top to go with hand-pressed soursop juice, just couldn't pass the gullet of anyone who tried to brave the dampening effects.

The whole village was in mourning, and the condolence-givers suspected that the headache was not like a passing dark cloud, that would normally go away after nine days. Victor's body was buried where he was bitten, and that added more salt to the wound. How could Vic have worked for a rich place, but his bones rotted somewhere else apart from where he was born? Was it for want of money to foot the bill? It baffled everybody, but each guess was as good as another, since high rollers coming back from abroad gave the impression that it was just a case of winning some and losing others.

"May I have your attention ladies and gentlemen? It's now almost 7:30, and we're directly over the J F Kennedy Airport." The captain gave us another voice piece that caused all to be all ears.

I looked through the window and it was still day. Quite out of line with Caribbean crepuscular hours that began as early as 5:30, sometimes 6:00 the latest. The mellowing evening sun, still some distance away from setting, cast a picturesquely nostalgic glow over a hustling and bustling creation below, and I picked up New York City like an eagle soaring high, while zooming in its prey.

The skyscrapers had me wondering how long it took planners to build what appeared to be an unmatched civilization. The *Twin Towers* stood out like a married couple, whispering a word of prayer for the rest of world. Cars resembling medium-sized boxes, crisscrossed along the way to make quadrangular locomotion, while utility poles looked more like toothpicks stuck in the ground by playful kids.

Flight 727 arrived at precisely the time predicted, and outside perhaps the largest airport in America, the air buzzed with busybodies. The operation was similar to any other major airline terminal that came to mind, only that this one was of a greater magnitude. I didn't hesitate in hailing a cab. But that was after noticing that all the operators jostling for the attention of exiting commuters were, in fact, every other race except black.

The driver of mine, a long-bearded, wrapped-headed male of Pakistani descent, was encaged in his little cubicle and engaged in some Punjabi or whatever language, crossed by interrupted radio signals along the way. The division was made possible by a partition that accommodated a small opening. The square hole was located almost immediately behind the back of his neck, where he could just turn his head slightly to obligingly exchange a word or two with his client, concerning destination or cash collection. We traveled in silence, except when the frequency of the communication contraption chipped in and out now and again. Meanwhile, the stranger, whose body language carried a message of each man for himself, headed for a hotel in Manhattan.

Sixty-five dollars a night was pretty expensive, but I felt like I had no choice, even to ask for a concession, after I finally got the front desk guy to give me a glance. It was like I never existed, even though I stood there before him for a good fifteen minutes, while he must have fixed all the loose papers behind the phone, tied his shoelace and put the gum wrapper in the trash.

"Oh, so this is where Miguel got the idea!" I connected the dots, gradually becoming conscious that I was perhaps going to be the only 'man of color' in the house, at least, for that night.

I was never accustomed to taking note of my complexion, or anybody else's for that matter, and where I came from, people weren't so conscious about skin-color. Comparatively speaking, it was like getting up everyday in the West Indies, not being worried about the weather and what it might bring. In those territories, it was almost a given expectation that the sun would come out, in a way that nobody thought about any inclement interference, until it finally happened. It was like a man, who didn't remember food until hunger struck.

However, there was a little touch of race issues in Jamaican elementary schools back in the seventies, when Indian kids were picked on, while stories circulated about their diet, weight and worth. But the ethnic group outlived that denigration, and integrated well until some grim reminder disturbed those individuals' unconsciousness.

Looking back, it must have been a nightmare for those indentured immigrants. However, thereafter they became history in a way that, nobody prolonged the agony about ethnicity, to even post an equal opportunity decree on paper.

The night I spent at that crappy, Cretaceous convenience was like an eternal evil inflicted on me, as a chastisement for something I did wrong. White drunkards paced the floors, bailing insults in English and other unfamiliar tongues, and the recognizable slurs were aimed straight at some unapproachable black encounters. Now, the only means of reprisal was for these vagabonds to vent their feelings, after consuming a few rounds, hoping that their dirty words weren't falling on deaf ears.

When I went to use the urinal, a few of the complainants converged inside the dilapidated restroom, and as soon as they felt my presence, they kept quiet, making me uneasy. The atmosphere in the bathroom was choking with the stench of vomit, and I quickly answered my call, before beating a hasty retreat. By then, my mind was already made up, that only a severe case of paralysis could make me spend another night at such a substandard stopover.

The Saturday morning was undetectable, if all I was depending on was a bird such as a nightingale, to get me in the right frame of mind. From the third floor, where the bellboy brought my things to hide me in a little attic-like room, clean enough to assure in retrospect that I had actually booked in a motel, I peered through the window for a good look at the streets of Manhattan. It was about 5:30, according to the timer on the cablevision apparatus, positioned on the night table between the headboards of the two single-sleeper beds, sparsely furnishing my dingy dwelling place.

Using my fingers to pull back the pleated, drape-like curtains, I could see two garbage trucks, as they emptied one dumpster after another. The procedure was so methodical and ingenious that I became cognizant of being indeed in a first-world country. The manner in which the scavengers did their thing, somewhat said a lot about what I used to hear on the side, that a street cleaner was better paid in these places than well known professionals in say, Jamaica.

The gamut of lights dismantled my memory of the morning stars. I didn't have to look towards the heavens for any semblance of wondrous attraction, unless I needed a reminder that the power on the face of this earth still rested in the hands of *The Supreme*. When I descended the stairs to get a good look outside, folks were still waiting in the lobby for one reason or another. However, I still didn't see anyone bearing my skin-type, and I became really concerned especially when I said *howdy do*, and nobody answered.

Out in the street I expected to come across some of my own kind, but when all luck seemed to vanish, I started walking a few blocks, forgetting to even take note of the street-name in case I got stranded. Just then, I looked at the keys with the details at hand, and quitted worrying. I had to hike about a hundred highways, before I saw a black man resembling a security guard, walking in the shadows of a myriad of white folks. I felt grateful that my prayer was answered, and that I finally found an oasis.

"Excuse me sir. Sorry to interrupt your duty." I tried to be as polite as possible, not to offend the only person in sight, who might be able to get my head around the confusion. "Where are the black people, if I might ask?"

The fellow looked me up and down, with a sort of distrusting apprehension flooding his face. That was something that struck me as a surprise, because I gave the introduction my all, not relying on our race to provide the base. I could tell that he was weighing his mind whether to yield to his good spirit, simply on account of wearing a uniform and badge. Perhaps he thought that that made him vulnerable to be reported, (as if that would have really mattered, given the circumstances of prevailing discrimination). Playing it safe, he sparingly shrugged his shoulders, before barely opening his lips, just so that a few words escaped.

"Go to Brooklyn," he muttered.

I had hoped that as two black people, though we had only just met, we were confident that, like dogs hunting in a pack, we were watching each other's back. Hence, we should have been able to talk about something that affected not only me, but also those who renamed themselves as African-Americans, such as those tokenized in high places. Instead, the officer wannabe kept walking, while I trotted behind, to put in another word or two.

"How do I get to Brooklyn?"

"Ride the subway."

I didn't want to look like a jackass, so I kept the rest of my reservations to myself. Obviously, this guy thought I had been in these places all my life, and he drew that conclusion by making very hasty assumptions. I found out later that drawing quick inferences was a fault that was the norm for the common folks. Miguel jumped the gun in San Juan, and now, within a day being in *The Big Apple*, the same disorder dominated.

I gathered my strength and decided to use my educational acumen, first staying calm and then observing. While walking, I saw an entrance that had letters and numbers, which I deciphered to be train symbols. I heard whirring under my feet. People were coming up breathlessly from below, where there was a hole in the ground, while others disappeared down under, running as if to catch a bus on the move. I followed the crowd, and found a whole new foundation underground, comparable to the busy conduits that connected movements above. I soon located the relevant train, and was on my way in a whistling wonder of the transportation world.

There was a sudden change, in that my train was full of black people interspersed with a good number of whites, a complete turnaround of my experience so far. I began to learn the ropes, figuring out that the United States was a united front. Consistently, I also realized that the name of the country was the indeed opposite, and an ironical epithet when it came to racial and quite frankly, other issues. As I said before, I was never the one to observe skin-color, until it slapped me in the face. However, in a train full of people with my hide-tone, I felt more comfortable than when I was so alone.

The ride rumbled on, stopping to let off and pick up passengers along the way. The automatic announcer alerted the seated and standing occupants about the stops and locations, both current and the ones approaching. Some travelers had earphones intact, enjoying audio entertainment. Many riders closed their eyes to avoid the stares from others sitting across from them on slippery, metallic benches that were yellow and orange in color. A desperate man came in, skipping across jerky and snaky train-cars, by squeezing his way through the limited doorway, before holding his breath for a while.

"Gentle people," he spoke up, way above the heads of his listeners. "I have AIDS, and I really don't mean to disturb your peace, but if you find it within your heart, you could make a donation to help with my medication," he implored, looking at me in particular.

I was shocked and scared, because I had heard about the deadly disease since it came about in the early or mid 80s, but had never blessed my eyes on any victim. Besides, I had hoped I would never come in contact with anybody, who signed that death sentence in any semblance. I took out a dollar and handed it to the speaker, all the time feeling uneasy, in this too-close-for-comfort encounter. Other individuals got busy finding spare change to make their contributions. I looked at their faces, and realized that they weren't worried about anything. I guessed it took a bit of getting used to the lifestyle, and the crowd showed that they had been down that road time and again.

After the unfortunate beggar forced his way to the next car, the air was relaxing once more. I remembered that my diary had numbers of close friends, who lived in the place I was bound for and was scheduled to reach in the next few minutes. Franco, my high school track coach, had migrated fifteen or so years aback. About a year before I knew I would have this kind of success in traveling, I saw him at the Jamaican stadium, while he was there for his yearly visit. He gave me his contact details, and told me to look him up if I ever took a trip. Judging from the way Franco sounded cocksure, I felt I shouldn't have a problem with somewhere to stop, even for a night, to get my feet on the ground.

The train finally made it to the Flatbush stop, and I hopped off like I was no stranger in town. I searched for a phone booth like someone with raw meat seeking fire. When I dialed Franco's number, luckily he was there to take the call, perhaps because age had slowed him down. The man I knew many moons before, was never a homeboy, and had never promised to become one anytime soon.

"Tommy is here too," Franco hastened to say, beating me to the punch before I could tell him my sad story.

The man with the once illustrious coaching career, tried to save himself the embarrassment from having to tell me he lived in a basement, and that I wouldn't be welcome even to spend an hour. Indirectly, he told me ahead of time that if I was about to get to the convenience part of my tale, by first stating my presence in his neighborhood, there was no real need for that, because he was not in a position to assist. The best he could do was to refer, and I had a choice to either take or leave it.

"Tommy!" I shouted in exhilaration. "Digits, my friend," I showed off my happier side. And Franco delivered before disappearing off the line.

Tommy was the one I needed to hear from, and it had been a lifetime since that hadn't happened. After our high school graduation, he was part of the almost entire school population, both before and after, that dispersed into these mainstreams without a trace. Everything was knitting together for my benefit, for more than one reason, now that his name came into the picture. First, hopefully he was in a position to remove me from the squalor in Manhattan, and second, being the star he was in those days, he could be the worldwide locator to keep me in touch with everybody else.

Tommy was glad to hear my voice, and why shouldn't he? We used to play together in school during our very junior years, and he had a kind of personality that was just not subject to changes, even with the toll of time. If anything, it had to be for the better. And I was about to find out, if this friend that I hadn't seen or heard from in so many years, could help me get there with my American dream. Could it be that my party was about to begin?

CHAPTER FOUR

Memories Going To The Grave

"Bruce Welds!" Tommy shouted my name in telepathic hilarity.

It didn't take him a split second to recognize me, even though it was the first time we spoke on the telephone, plus we hadn't heard each other in years. Perhaps he had good reasons to remember my voice so accurately, since we had a long history. I used to be on the run from Tommy, when he and his cousin Rod teamed up to kick my butt in several bouts of horseplay. We had fond memories going with us to the grave, and I remembered them like they happened as we spoke. There was this day in particular, when there was an incident that created so much excitement, the whole school laughed beyond its boundary.

It was lunchtime, and after a hearty meal of steamy-hot bread that melted the cheese, stuck in the middle of the round dough, the chase began after I got the better of Rod in a fake fight. That got Tommy on the defensive. Rod was really in my class, so we were virtually the same age.

But Tommy, who was like two years our senior, decided to go after me like Goliath getting a go at David. I ran from the challenge and bolted down the bottom playfield, which was deeply forested, due to being left fallow for months. That area was a sharp drop of a few meters from the top, where the school building with corridors reminiscent of a stadium seating arrangement at match-time, overlooked the main soccer field.

The sun was in ship shape, and the breeze swayed the knee-level grasses into a pattern, where the leaflets leaned on each other. Kids converged in different groups under lignum vitae trees that made good shades for the sweating students. Meanwhile, the guys made soccer balls out of empty juice boxes, kicking them around to entertain themselves, while they awaited the sound of the school bell.

I was meters away from the chase pack, which had grown to about four. Then I felt something unusual underneath my pants, just below my left knee. Still half-running, I grabbed that part of my trousers in the palm of one hand, and felt an organism the shape of a lizard. When it wriggled under pressure from my fingers, I knew I was right.

"Help!" I cried out, hoping for some leniency. "A lizard in my pants!" I was both tired and disheveled.

By then, all the other boys had gained on me, and were now only inching closer to gloat at my distress.

"Where is it?" one of them asked, intending to discredit my cry, just in case I had wanted to pull a fast one.

Meanwhile, I held on to the cold-blooded creature, and felt it writhing like it was begging to be released from its prison. I feared letting it go, in which case, it might turn around and run in the wrong direction to create further ridicule. I squeezed the life out of it, and then shook my leg to watch, as did everyone else, while a dark brown reptile fell to the ground from under my crisply ironed khaki. That didn't stop Tommy from giving me a couple clouts, but our romp came to an abrupt end. By then the school bell had rung, and we had to make it to the line out in the courtyard. Failing to make that 'deadline' carried its own penalties, and from experience, we knew it was not worth the risk to get there late.

Those were the good old days, and Tommy surely had an irrefragable recollection of my voice from back then.

"Where are you?" My friend obviously knew I was out of Jamaica, when he saw the Brooklyn number registered on his Caller ID, but he only wanted specifics.

"At a public phone in Flatbush," I quickly replied, to greet him with my desperation while I still had the chance. "I slept in a rat-hole last night in Manhattan, and I need your help," I traded my voice of open petition.

"Go get your things and meet me at the Gun Hill Road train station. Call me when you get there." He was assuming I knew my way around, but that was okay.

After exchanging a bit of laughter that promised a happy reunion, we got off the line and I got busy with my research. Common sense told me to retrace my steps, which included employing a little knowledge. I landed on one platform. Therefore I needed to cross over to the other side, to take the same kind of train back to my starting point. That was what I did, and in no time I was back at the hotel, packing like there was no more tomorrow.

I took my stuff downstairs, where I asked the porter for an emergency call, and told Tommy I was heading his way. My longtime pal was in Bronx, and I had to take the same D train to get to him. The only difference was that the tunnel speedster would travel northbound this trip.

I was Bronx-bound in a jiffy, being in such a glee to see what this buddy of mine looked like after all those years. So many things washed ashore, when I thought about those times when he was a central figure in school. That ranged from one blast from the past in track-and-field half-lap, quarter-mile and other middle distance races, to his womanizing ways.

I couldn't forget that Sports Day, when there was nobody to run the 200m senior boys for my *House*, and Tommy, being the jack of all trade, was down to fill the gap. When the field lined up behind their blocks, all eyes were fixed on this powerfully built athlete, with veins conspicuously streamlining his members. He was obviously the crowd's favorite, who was also a prime representative at the national championships.

"The camel called," someone shouted from the taunting throng. "He wants his lungs back." That was just to say that the lapper was out of his league.

In fact, perhaps Tommy didn't remember that he was in a sprint race, and that since he was running with a heavy weapon, chances were he needed a sturdy protective shield. And for a little bit of briefing, everybody had to shower in the locker room after a class of physical education or athletic training, under normal conditions. Hence, it was an open secret that that boy was armed and dangerous in the penile department.

That 200m race was the hilt of the running events. The distant-runner-turned-sprinter got off to a blistering start, and either his jockstrap gave way under the weight, or there was none save a boxer to begin with. But coming off the bend, the tough cookie was running on three visible legs.

"Flip, flop, flip, flop," the one in the middle was beating the two on its outside like a stirrup, to get them going.

Laugher spoiled, as the core of cheerleaders and spectators braced against the guard ropes, to get a close-up shot of the fearless forerunner. Meanwhile, Tommy couldn't afford to let down *Sherlock House* that he stood for, and finished the race in fine style, before putting his organ back where it belonged. Needless to say, a winner like that had the girls bowing at his feet, no pun intended.

While I sat on the train, I could only imagine that Tommy was married with kids, in fulfilling the aspirations of someone destined to become the guy next-door, when it came to family life. The train traversed high and low grounds. Sometimes it drove fear into my heart, when I looked down through cracks and crevices, to see the crowns of pedestrians, as they went in and out of distorted corner stores. The vehicle stopped at every station, and at times it hesitated in mid-earth, causing restlessness among passengers, who seemed to be going home after a hard day, nine to five.

Then the stringy carrier lulled to a halt, and it was the Gun Hill Road location. I disembarked with my boring baggage, and ascended the stairs, before passing through a one-way token-operated gateway. The station was strategic in its position at the side of a hill. But down below, the aged tracks translated an eerie kind of existence, shutting out the afternoon sun, while commuters waited on both sides.

The Gun Hill Road port opened on to the motorway, resonating well with business ventures. Those ranged from taxi service to Laundromats, while the weekend caterers stirred up the appropriate ambience. The sun spread a kind of colorful glow, that gave the appearance of Saturday in some rural parts of Jamaica during the nostalgic seventies, when *Oldies But Goodies** were aired throughout the day.

As soon as I entered the piazza, where black taxi operators stood waiting to get a break, something both liquid and softly solid went 'plop', on my shaved head, spilling all over me in a second. My white shirt was so flooded, that the material displayed the full dose of pigeon excrement that caught me flush. I stopped in my track, not knowing what move to make, with the mess dribbling like tears down the trenches on my face. Then I realized that the station roof-gutters were the home of dozens of domestic doves.

"That's good luck. You're a lucky man," said a taxi chauffeur encouragingly. He noticed that I was stupefied. Perhaps he hoped that by helping me with a napkin, I might end up in his waiting minivan that was among a string of transportations with the same purpose, lining the side of Gun Hill Road. When I looked across the street from where the bird disencumbered its bowels on my shoulders, Tommy was sitting in his 1998 Dodge Ram, waiting to make my life a little easier.

He saw everything that happened, and took my nasty experience one step further.

"Your kind of drama just never seems to end," he chuckled.

He jumped out of the brand-name bus that wore the tag of his personality. We embraced in the warm breeze of the open suburban street, which had residential homes beginning from its adjacent Wilson Avenue fork-like intersection, where he parked. It took us a while to set each other free, and after packing my things in his spacious ride, we set off towards home, hoping to catch up on a lot in comfort.

I wanted to ask him about his personal life, while we took it easy along the way, but I thought I would let Tommy volunteer the information. He apparently chose to delay my astonishment for the moment when we entered his one-bedroom apartment, which contained facilities fit for a single king.

"Surprise, surprise, surprise," he said. "You thought you'd see a woman here now, right? Wrong!" he contradicted, as if he read my mind. However, although he declared that he had toned down on his lascivious lifestyle as a lady's man, I was left to learn that living solo boosted his inclination towards multiple flings. And Tommy explained how he happened to stage this one-man show.

He had actually only begun going it alone and loving it, a year before I got there. Prior to that, he was shacking up with Sharon, who he described as psycho when jealousy took control of her mind, body and soul. According to him, he couldn't speak to his own cousin, without having a lot of explanations ready to redeem himself from all kinds of accusations. Neither he nor his fiery girl had any exclusive rights to the four-bedroom flat, for which they both split the costs. However, Sharon begged to differ.

"One day I came home to find my belongings at the gate, and I was shown the door," Tommy disclosed.

That spoke volumes for why he was resolute to be by himself, albeit on conditions of conditionality. Now, this was one man with a well-rounded personality, and he was just as formidably explosive as he was known to be the *Mr. Nice Guy*. Apparently, on that occasion, Tommy knew when to walk away and when to run. And wishing to stay in control, he intentionally found the single-occupancy space to entertain female guests, one night at a time.

I couldn't help observing a lot about my host's busy biography during my first week of stay. But I wasn't in any way appalled - a leopard never changed its spots. The telephone rang off the hook, and it was like this lover-boy had a roster of names that he flipped through, reminiscing on the last flings to see which one sent his libido in overdrive. He perhaps made a shortlist even! If the prime selection didn't call, then he would do her the favor, and the recipient of his summons felt privileged to come knocking.

I got to meet Sharon under a similar *she-loves-me-not-she-loves-me* game plan. One late evening, she showed up unannounced, after the big man was booked to have Julie stay a little while longer for dessert. He had already had his main course, when the middle-aged passerby whetted his appetite in the bathroom.

I mainly stayed home for the first few days because I never knew anywhere to go. Furthermore, Tommy was taken up with work, plus as I said, his private life. I sat on the sofa in the living room, while the *call girl* and her man made out on the only bed in the whole accommodation.

The bedroom door was ajar, and I could see foot movements at work. A few male toes pushed for the closure of the plywood framework, to get some form of privacy. Essentially, that was difficult to achieve, in light of the existing architecture. They perhaps didn't want to insult my intelligence, and therefore pretended to have unfinished business to address in the bathroom.

About ten minutes after their disappearance, the telephone rang, and the person was calling for the man of the house.

"Tom," I shouted, pretending that I was unaware of the height of ecstasy that must have been overcoming him at that moment.

"Take a message. Take a message," he replied, catching his breath between each word, in the throes of the orgasmic order that was getting the better of his involuntary vulnerability.

It was Sharon, and although she didn't make an appointment when Tommy was too busy to come to the phone, an hour or so later, she was at the door. By then, Tommy was relaxing with Julie waiting for a second round.

The polygamist remained calm under the existing circumstances, and so did the competitors, as both females put on a show of good manners in light of my presence as a stranger. The man in the middle simulated that the two ladies were just casual companies, and in response, both complied as if they were compelled by some unknown undercurrents. Sharon knew she was walking on chalk-line, given the probation on which she was leashed, and Julie was married with her nursing profession to protect.

The latter sat on a chair on one side of the living room, while Sharon who heard so much about me in the past, impressed that we were the best of friends. The woman, who used to be Tommy's live-in lady, made her bid to psychologically oust any hopes from the head of this 'newcomer', who she was now only just seeing in the picture.

The faces of both girls showed each couldn't wait for the other to leave, and as for Sharon, it was a matter of getting to the bottom of what was in the air. However, Julie mainly had that look of readiness to ride along on the bathroom floor, where she had had her eyes all set to topple again with Tommy, before she was unpleasantly intercepted.

It was 10:00 0'clock and they were still there. Julie resorted to reading a magazine to while away the hours, while Sharon was still attempting to make an impression under my elbows. Meanwhile, Tommy stayed inside the bedroom, and acted as though he didn't give two hoots about the rivalry, that I was left to handle in this unfamiliar situation. Eleven o'clock, twelve, one, two, three.

The married woman left after she perhaps smelled the rat that she was putting her family on the line. And by then, Sharon had gone into the bedroom, shamming that she was helping to straighten the mess, left behind by the one she had only just outlasted. I fell asleep on the sofa and the rest was history.

At the end of my first exciting week in Bronx, Rod called his cousin to wish him happy *Father's Day*, and Tommy arranged a conference.

"Bruce is here!"

"What? Put him on!" Rod demanded.

I returned the favor to point the *Father's Day* adoration in Rod's direction. We spoke for a long time about old times, emphasizing that our last eye-to-eye meeting was ten years before in Half-Way-Tree. He had migrated shortly after, courtesy of a filing done by Charles, his estranged father. The latter had taken up residency in *The States* immediately before Rod was born, but had never returned to look at the two boys he left with Precious, the mother of them both.

While attending high school, the two brothers and their cousin stuck together like the three little pigs, boarding the school-bus everyday. But Precious was the single mom behind the harmonious appearance, while Charles was gone and forgotten.

Like Tommy, they both had the girls weak in the knees. But Rob, Rod's brother, who was the same age as Tommy, led the way as the player in many admirers' estimation. Rob was blessed with brain too, and immediately after high school, he got his degree in Civil Engineering. Then Charles set up his firstborn with the least a dad could do for a son, to let him go after his American dream. The young immigrant subsequently got married to a woman of Trinidadian roots, intending to set up a successful family.

Rod, on the contrary, was married from the day we started high school, at least so we all thought, when his devotion to Bev went all the way up to graduation. At the prom, his first love was pregnant with his son, and the young mom-to-be continued to have eyes only for him, like she was endowed with the whale syndrome**. However, when the camera was off, Rod got involved with someone else, which left a lot of us with our mouths wide open.

Bev didn't give up hopes, and never spoke to another man since the mistrust. Instead, she entertained the thought that some day she would hear a knocking at her door, and it would turn out to be the love of her life. It didn't matter if he went to the mighty USA, where aggressive women would most likely have swooped down on his good looks, like flies going after sugar. The perfectly built six-footer would be coming back home where his heart was buried.

By the time Rod made it to Miami to join his sibling, Rob was in a position to take him in, at least until Joanna, Rob's wife, nagged that Rod needed to pack his things and leave. After the standoff threatened the survival of the marriage, Rod surrendered. That led the younger brother to shack up with Jenny, his new girlfriend, to split the costs of the apartment that came to his rescue. The graphic artist held down a job as a disc jockey with his tremendous talent, and was pretty secure that he was good enough to go.

When we spoke, he was just getting on his feet, and was looking forward to even greater things. He was weaned perhaps untimely, but with a brilliant display of artistry at one of Florida's prime radio stations, who needed a father, or even a brother, who yielded to his wife's wishes to kick him out in the streets?

One week to the date that we had the conference call, and Tommy was still up to no good with his harem, I woke up to hear a loud, gut-wrenching telephone conversation between my homeboy and someone on the other end of the line. It was three o'clock dawn time, and I was still dazed, just getting out of the deep sleep that I had fallen into, while watching a movie. Actually, I was lying prostrate on the bed that must have grown accustomed to so much rocking and knocking.

Tommy did not wake me up to take my place on the all-purpose sofa-bed out in the living room, and

I didn't even know when I started snoring, until his voice got me out of it. I remained with my eyes closed, still under the influence of deep dozing. I wanted to know what was causing the anxiety in the dialogue, and yet, I felt too powerless to probe. Then suddenly, I was forced to get involved.

"Bruce, Bruce," Tommy insisted, trying to get my attention, after he perhaps noticed that I had shaken a little

"Yes," I responded, feeling very concerned.

"Rod is dead."

"What!" I rolled the sheet from over my face, and sprang to my feet, sitting up on the bed in a silly shock. After all, it was my former classmate he was talking about, and a very famous one at that.

The darkest part of the night was when that Tuesday was about to dawn, and I wished for the sun to come sooner than it would. It was as still as a tomb in the surrounding apartments littering that dead-end street on Mickle Avenue. The mood measured up with something magically transplanted from a horror film, in which two unbelievers were left to face a fact that was so irreversible.

Tommy wept uncontrollably, and I knew he was not kidding. I hadn't seen a macho guy holler in a long time, if at all I had ever seen one. By now, he had cut off the caller, and began to wash away the room with his relentless sobs. Then he told me the whole story that was to change the course of our short-lived reunion, and supposedly, the way he would go about the rest of his life.

Hardly had Rod moved in with his new girlfriend of convenience, when he ran into Pam. The latter was part of the original core of forty-two from high school, when Faith had needed an audience. After graduation, everybody scattered and it had been a decade and a half that Pam and Rod hadn't been in touch. She had found him irresistible from way back then, but with Bev in the way, she kept her distance.

They exchanged numbers, but Rod exercised scant regard for the effect that that would have had on his live-in lover, perhaps because as little more than housemates, they didn't share the same alma mater. Whereas he had almost grown up with Pam, he had scarcely been with Jenny for six months. And that was like having to make adjustments, which took time that he didn't really have to spare.

It turned out that he really needed to invest a lot more years to get to know Jenny. He perhaps would have discovered that unlike Bev, she was not someone to leave high and dry. One fatal telephone call was all it took to shake up the community of Montgomery Park, where Morant Bay High had its plethora of past people.

Rod might not have given Pam his work schedule, or more information about his sleeping arrangement. Perhaps the latter was calling to fill in the blanks with what they didn't have time to do, when they crossed path in a hurry at that shopping mall. Whatever the contagion, everyone familiar with the troubled connection, cursed the minute the three made it into a triangle.

"Hello," Jenny began, after picking up the phone. Nobody answered. She lost the caller but decided to *star sixty-nine* the number, and sure enough, it was a woman just like she had thought. "Did you call this line a minute ago?"

"Yes, who are you?"

"You called! Who *are* you?"

"Is this Rod's number?"

"Bitch, why are you asking for my man?"

"Honey, Rod and I have come a long way, and you won't come between us. Again, who are you?"

"If that's the case, we will sort this out once for all. Hold the line, please."

And Jenny proceeded to call the guy, who she thought she had possessed monogamously. Then she reached for a foot-long kitchen knife that she placed under her pocketbook.

"Rod, oh my God! Someone is breaking in the house, and I don't know what to do. Please, please come home now!" She supplicated and whispered, doing so in a tense tone that caused Rod to fear the worst.

It was only thirty minutes left to call it a night on his late-night shift, and hence he asked for permission to get off the air. Home was ten minutes away, but like a bird taking its find to feed its young, he was there in five. Rod looked around, and estimated that his house was safe enough that he could enter, without putting his life at risk. And so, he went in and shut the door behind him.

"Jenny, are you okay?" he enquired, and pertinently doing so because he heard her talking on top of her voice.

Jenny ran downstairs with the phone in her hand. Pam was still on the line, while the extremely jealous and armed woman advanced towards the man of the moment.

"Here," said Jenny, and she stretched the receiver for Rod to take control of it.

The unsuspecting boyfriend didn't see the dagger, strapped surreptitiously under the radius of his lady's right hand that she held by her side, while he complied. Like a tragic scene from *Romeo and Juliet*, she feigned delivering the calling instrument, before plunging the weapon deep inside his torso, as if she sent an arrow straight through his heart.

Blood gushed out of his aorta like water from a broken fire hydrant. Meanwhile, Rod turned back impulsively through the door, collapsing on the steps of the pair's fifteen-hundred-dollars-a-month residence. He howled as life left his body, and the serum of the human being watered the lawn like it came from a flushing hose, doing so until his veins ran dry.

All that time, Pam heard the ordeal from her end, especially when Rod's voice went dead, and knew that something had just happened that was about to make headlines. She called the cops, just in time as Jenny jumped to her feet to find a defense.

The hell-bent, bloodthirsty woman also got the cops to listen to a story she concocted, that Rod was engaging her in his usual domestic violence. However, she was oblivious to the call made by a taxi operator, who had witnessed the giant body that bolted through the door, before slumping onto the stairs outside. The three different sets of officers that turned up on the scene, investigated the case, and changed the charge to second-degree murder, to match the overriding evidence.

At daybreak the overnight news had numbed both of us, and although two heads should have been better than one, neither one had the faintest clue how to move forward. Neighbors jumped around as usual, some getting behind their wheels, while others hurried towards their nearest bus stop on either Baychester Avenue or Boston Road.

Little by little, the hustlers increased their presence on these main streets, panhandling or looking for the slightest opportunity to exploit somebody's misfortune. Many Jamaicans were among those who loitered and paraded in shady areas, watching both the human and vehicular traffic to single out, or even double their chances of going home with something at sunset.

Meanwhile, the story grew wings, and Bev was the first to get wind of the epic tragedy. Now, she had to live with the horrific reality, that the man she had given a long rope, had used it to hang himself. Her tenth-grade son was now fatherless, and everything happened so senselessly when least expected. She was left with the inexorably dirty duty to break the painful grief to the loved ones, especially Rod jr. and Precious, who were in one place at the time.

Bev took a taxi to make it to them in one whole. Precious was in the kitchen preparing breakfast for her grandson, when her daughter-in-law-hopeful entered without a knock. Sensing that something never seemed right, she stopped turning the ripe plantain in the frying pan. Then she searched the untimely visitor's face for something to console herself that all was well. But alas, she found nothing!

"It's about Rod in USA," Bev broke down. "He's gone," she continued. There was no easier way to melt down the news to the elderly woman.

Precious turned off the fire under the cooker, and instinctively, both women reached for each other, for a shoulder on which to lean. Grandma was too distraught to even cry. Meanwhile, Bev gave her the sketch she had, of how everything transpired. The tension compounded as a result of the distance between the dead man and the people who really mattered. Besides, it was not like the two women, or even Rod's son, possessed a visa to board the next flight to Miami for some first-hand information.

Charles needed to chime in to get this chagrin out of the way. But where responsibility was concerned, relying on this man to respond to the crisis was more like depending on President Bush to withdraw the American troops from Iraq in due course. Precious would be the fittest one to stand up in court to seek justice for the son she spent her last energy to raise. The high-profile case could do without a fictitious father, who regarded it a favor to even give the undertaking fifty percent of his commitment. And so, the aftermath of the insane slaughter radiated towards different tangents, setting up a showdown that highlighted stress in capital letters.

Despite all the overcast days ahead, I had to look past those setbacks to focus on my way forward. I had run too many races where competitors fell inches away from my most recent stride, and I had to ignore the downfall and look for the finish line. Although I was going to be left out in the cold when Tommy left to attend the funeral in Jamaica, I told myself that one closed door would open up a million more in motion.

I had another week to think about that action-reaction inspiration, to decide how I was going to be defibrillated out of this state of shock. I remembered my father's famous words: '*walk for no reason is better than stay home for nothing*'. Hence, I started leaving the house.

I wandered on Baychester Avenue, wondering why these events were like pouring egg-white in a glass of water on *Good Friday*. One just never knew how things were going to shape up, and the eventual pattern in the liquid might simply be somebody's superstitious statement.

A blackbird came into view, watching me directly as if to empathize with my difficulties. The sidewalk cut its own track for a mile or two along the main road, and the fleet-footed, shine-eyed hopper chose to skip along with me to a section, where a small forest made a little recreation park across from Spellman High School. Beastly schoolboys dunked shots in loops, raucously tugging at each other on a basketball court a little way down.

While the adult bird made sure to keep abreast, I observed that she seemed to look at me playfully, while jumping towards the inner part of the bushes. I went for the game, and stepped towards her jokingly too. She leapt another couple of inches inward, and I did the same. She toyed with the idea, doing a couple more steps, until we were inside a little thicket. Right there in the tall, green, savannah-type grass, a ten-dollar bill winked at me.

Nobody would have discovered that dough, based on its position. But there it was, at the right place to rejuvenate my peace of mind. Obviously, my luck was turning around with something as small as that, and I was grateful for it like a crack-addict kissing a quarter. Indeed, I had been using up my reserves, without any foreseeable replenishment. I thanked the bird, and she flew away after she was satisfied that the cash was safe in my hands.

I started counting my blessings to invigorate my willpower, instead of surrendering to adversities. Two days later, I felt like clearing my brain. I left Mickle Avenue to tread along my lucky path, again not knowing what to expect. The sun was still striking hot, when I completed my trip and was heading back home, believing that my afternoon was going to be uneventful.

As I crossed at the stoplight monitoring the intersection between Boston Road and Baychester Avenue, the light switched to green. I had to hurry to best the crazy cars that raced down like they were brake-less. In the middle of the crosswalk, stood a crumpled paper. Though the traffic was pretty much on my back, I risked it to turn around, grabbed the garbage-seeming material, and ran out of the way with my life in my hands. While the curious drivers rubbernecked to figure out my find, I straightened out what I slowly thought was a dollar, to enjoy the sight of fifty times that amount. I raised it towards the heavens and kissed it hello.

I stopped at a restaurant on the spot, where access to a public phone was immediate. My effort was to contact a high school friend, who had been giving Tommy moral support since the tragedy. I was in a glee to tell her about my pluses, and so I started dialing her number.

Just as I completed the dial-up using the old-fashioned equipment, I looked down at my feet, while I waited for Dawn to pick up. I was almost standing on twenty dollars! I jumped at the cash, and quickly forgot about everything else. Those increments told me that my American dream could get on the right track, if I simply learned how to claim it.

* Music of the past
** Whales mate with one partner for life

CHAPTER FIVE

Permit My American Dream

"Eighty dollars in three days!" Dawn exclaimed. "I've been here for fifteen years and not even a dime," she explained, not realizing that she was strengthening my resilience and tenacity by merely confirming that everybody's road was different. That meant I should be more concerned about what I brought to the table, rather than looking at the failures of other immigrants.

Dawn was the A-student in our time at Morant Bay, and when she opted for greener pastures promptly after graduation, we all thought her dream was to lecture somewhere in a university in Harvard's category. Thanks to Rod's passing, I became aware that she was a part of the Bronx community, living a few streets away from Mickle Avenue. Hence, the day after I doubled the pleasure, picking up what generous losers left behind, I found myself in the house of my best female friend in the past. Sissy, her mom, was there too, and had not even a single gray hair to show that she had seven kids, one as old as Tommy.

Dawn was married with two boys, and her husband was a part of the US Navy. Hence, she could afford to be a full-time housewife, while collecting sizeable allowances from the US government. However, she kept up a nomadic lifestyle, and during the bereavement, was getting ready to settle in Alaska according to the mandates imposed on her army man.

" I thought you had become a diplomat," I said to the lady, who used to collect the majority of the subject prizes as a junior.

"My mom stayed home and raised all her kids. I think I owe that commitment to mine too, especially in times and places like these," she replied to justify why she hadn't been using the advanced degree she got, since transplanting in the late seventies.

Dawn had gained a few pounds and looked a little different from her youthful distinction. While she baked the chicken to serve with macaroni and cheese, I sat on the kitchen stool wondering whether I was seeing her double. She still had a touch of beauty, but time had done its own alterations. It was evident that her eating habits made all the difference, being geared towards the average American taste buds. I examined her physique, and remembered when American children used to spend holidays in Jamaica. The big kids looked more like giants when they stood beside the local simpletons, who were sometimes even older than the visitors.

The flavor of the menu gave her the credit that she had a first degree in being a dietician. But her two boys demonstrated the obedience and training of a mother who had really tried her best at installing the first principles of comportment.

In the USA, daycare nurseries gave millions of mothers the freedom to find their niche. On the contrary, the kids paid for this with unhealthy upbringing, while enduring abuses of all sorts that set them up to be the generation of vipers. In light of this observation, Dawn selflessly gave over her life to serving her family. However, like a lot of other immigrants, she seemed to have lost the zeal to utilize the academic talent that she demonstrated in her youthful years.

Contrastingly, it was Sissy who stole the show with her usual radiance! Not even a tinge of that catwalk composure appeared to have disappeared. I met her on *Parent Day* during my third year of high school, and she looked like Miss World wanted to meet her. Now, after some eighteen or so years, the model mom was still fit for Broadway.

On that day that I showed up unexpectedly on the doorsteps of their two-family house, the three of us took the bus to town, leaving the other members of the extended family at home. While I played the perfect gentleman to let mother and daughter ascend first on board, I wondered how many people could have pointed out which of the two women brought the other into the world, without having to take a second guess.

Sissy was the one who promised to get her best friend to take me in, when Tommy said it was against his lease to leave a third party in place, while he went to bury his cousin. I wanted to open different doors to my success. I started looking around for other options, while Sissy had to wait for her girl's green light. However, that was contingent on the fact that that friend's American husband had a say in the decision.

One gate gaped at me in Connecticut in a place called Wethersfield. I found the number of a professor of Special Chemistry, who taught at the University of the West Indies some time in the 1990s, while I was a senior at that institution. His name was Rick, a seventy-odd-year-old white American research wizard, introduced to me by one of his students, who was my training partner. Like Franco, Rick had given me his impersonal invitation to *The States*, even before I dreamt that Barry would swallow the bait to supply me with my boarding pass. The good thing was that this senior citizen had the first-world title, and nothing could change that, even if he switched allegiance to become a homegrown terrorist.

I fled the Bronx with the strange feeling that I would be back, but left behind a lot of emotional distress pouring in from all corners. Pam was pummeled for causing the friction that fueled the fatal fracas. Tommy was taken up with trampling Rob for allowing his wife to send Rod packing. And seeking justice was going to be another complicated story with a plot fit for a film. Travel arrangements to get Rod's body to Retreat in St. Thomas demanded an arm and a leg. Plus people had given up valuable work hours, which could cost them dearly in the final analysis. Meanwhile, the Morant Bay Alumni Association was bubbling with its own agenda. I really needed to get away from this melting pot of mayhem, now that I got a clearer meaning of the life's-too-short cliché.

Rick drove to pick me up all the way from his hometown, glad to be associated with someone who he claimed reminded him of his face-to-face camaraderie with the wonderful West Indian hospitality. Supposedly at his age, it was ordinary for most people to show their greatest appreciation for the simpler things life had to offer, and Rick was simply grateful to be alive firing on all his faculties.

The road to Connecticut passed through green vegetations consisting of pine and other softwood medley, and strong breeze whistled through the weeping willows.

"Where are the fruit trees?" I asked, searching for those that children normally loved.

"Fruit trees? Man, you must be out of your mind! You're not in Jamaica!"

Eternal plains, lined with forests that had deer and black bears hurrying across the lonely heat-glistening highway, made me imagine what it felt like, picking up a puncture or worse, have a dead car to worry about in this wilderness. It was like, if we stopped to even change tires, we could expect a monster to pounce from out of nowhere, to make the mechanical failure the least of our concerns.

We must have traveled another eighty miles, before buildings started to peek at us piece by piece from a distance, and before long we were in Hartford. An extremely picturesque and thickly populated capital, I fell in love with it a first sight.

We stopped for a little sightseeing, during which Rick pointed to Princeton College located in proximity, and as a current lecturer there, he called the town his second home. We lingered for a while to watch the Friday evening crowd tripping over itself, before we headed for the outskirts of that very modern metropolitan meeting place.

Twenty minutes later we were in Wethersfield, with its reinvented country houses and unlocked land space, that had no visible surveyor's seal to say where each neighbor couldn't dare. All the constructions were the same color, and the grassy lawns seemed to tell the story of a midsummer night's dream. It was as though the occupants were so happy to have the warm season, that to cut the shrubs would have been an act of desecration.

Rick pulled up in his unbridled driveway, where I could practically see the living silence permeating the houses in a contagious link, and it was pretty obvious each landowner was discretely another's keeper. Nightfall began to paint a picture of solitude, when most of the intellectually-oriented night-owls drew their curtains to forget about their exterior surroundings.

Rick helped me to haul my things inside his two-story dwelling that was equipped with facilities for all times. The living room had a fireplace with clean, antique fuel and firewood in their appropriate places, and never seemed to miss the touch of his deceased wife in the large family picture on the wall. In the framed photo, her eyes seemed vividly bright as if to say in death, they were still open to oversee what went on in the house. And though the children had all gone to have a life of their own, Rick felt compelled to carry on as if nothing had changed.

Once the door was closed, a sudden state of loneliness overcame my emotions, and as the gray-haired host beckoned me towards the kitchen, I felt like crying. We sat around the kitchen table that looked like since the day his wife succumbed to breast cancer, it longed to hear the clinkering of utensils to keep it serving its purpose.

"Cheer up," Rick said, when he noticed a teardrop rolling down my cheek.

"Homesickness."

I passed it off as something that could be overcome. However, if Rick only knew that I was carrying the world on top of my shoulders, maybe he would have understood that only a breakthrough could have made a world of difference on my side. I tried to brush away the signs of my discomfort.

Just then, Rick got up and drew back a sliding glass-door to get to his garden. He pulled up a few stalks of lettuce and a cabbage, whose foliage barely overlapped. Then he picked some tomatoes. I could tell he was proud of his green thumb, as he returned inside to place some bagels in a microwave, before taking out plates and forks to set the old wooden table. I didn't feel like eating, since I needed more time to trust the cleanliness of his existence, especially given that he served the vegetables without applying a drop of cold water to them.

I nibbled at bits and morsels of Rick's entrée, just to save myself some embarrassment, while the culinary master slurped away at the contents, like his fingers needed to be careful. It seemed I had to get comfortable with the idea that for the next how long, this was what my meals were going to entail. I knew that when I went somewhere for the first time, it usually took a while for a little adjustment to anchor. But I searched the present and beyond, yet only felt overwhelmed deep inside.

The room Rick placed me after a brief tour of his very comfortable den, had everything to make me feel at home on the uppermost floor. However, I found it difficult to connect with the aura, which tugged at my élan with the might of a depression. I made it through the night, sleeping with the lights as bright as the illumination of the bulbs of an Olympic stadium. In the morning, I went to the breakfast table going through the motions.

I prayed for the weekend to pass and it did. Rick had to be in school in Hartford, and I arranged with him to leave me in town and pick me up on his way back. My Monday sparkled a lot while I took my own sweet time to peruse the city. Then I stumbled upon a park, where a carousel was the major attraction for kids on their summer recess.

Side benches filled up at the sound of brilliant chiming and rhyming, while joggers cruised by at their own speed to peek at the infant performances. Across from this stellar entertainment, the streets were on their own mission, some marked with single-entry signs to control the steady flow of traffic. The crowd that used them was a jubilant mixture of black, brown, yellow and white faces, sometimes jumbled in assorted variations. If there were any tension among these bystanders, it was certainly not visible from the standpoint of an outsider.

The *YMCA* stood in the mix just meters away, erected on the brow of where the built-up ground began to rise, helping to supply the park with people of various interests. Further up, the *Civic Center* showed off its wide range of sleeping steps. The rungs challenged the lungs of anyone who thought this ascending order in terracing was easy to climb, until the bidder found out that one flight could easily become his quota of exercise for one day. The fast food caterers hovered in the background, as if to anticipate the needs of a population, that was sure to crave just about anything edible to fill a hungry void.

Back in the park, foot-patrolling guards made their presence poignant, occasionally getting up from under one of the towering, hollow-trunk trees that encircled the acres of grassy plains, where singles and couples rolled to relax from a ripping mid-morning sun. The informal officers wearing bluish-gray, short pants to go with matching shirts and helmets, mingled with the active park population, but didn't deter the exhibitionists that also perambulated the circumference looking for easy targets.

The days that followed were solidly similar, and I ran into a few interesting characters that kept me occupied until my ride arrived. I was about to call it a fruitful week of frolic where, if it were all up to me, I would have perhaps hesitated in the area to see if my dream was earmarked to connect in Connecticut. However, on the eighth day of my stay in Wethersfield, something strange happened.

It was Friday in mid-June and I must have slept later than Rick could wait to chauffeur me to town that morning. He left a note describing how to get the tri-hourly transport that plied the prejudiced pasture of car-owning people. When I found out I was the only one in the house that had not fully caught my scent, I hurriedly washed myself and dashed off into the streets to catch the carrier.

I had to walk a few blocks to the nearest bus stop. I passed many houses without seeing anybody even try to pick up a twig, or pull up a weed from a front yard. My mind was fused with the will to find my way, when I saw about five puzzled-looking white women, converged on their lawn on the upcoming block. It wasn't clear what they were doing, since my retina was resolved to respect their privacy, reducing them to mere objects rather than real people, as far as my optical monitor was programmed.

As I neared the mini, nimble-mouthed gathering, they walked briskly towards the doorsteps of their bungalow, and that was when I actually focused my lenses on the moving Neanderthals. Then a second thought appeared to have occurred to one of them, and she stopped. All that time, I was still unaware that I was the reason for the press conference that was in the act of disintegrating.

"Excuse me!" the one with the birdbrain shouted over her shoulders. "Are you the gas man?"

"No," I replied, without even thinking to get a good look at the nincompoop behind the shrilly voice.

The woman, plus the others who braked up to hold their breath for my response, took off again like they heard news. That was when it registered that I was the monster that was chasing them. I continued as if nothing happened, after the lunatics loaded themselves behind their closed door. Nevertheless, I hoped that Wethersfield wasn't really reflected in what just went wrong.

Once again, I enjoyed Hartford, but I had a hard time putting the morning's mishap to death. When Rick came to get me that afternoon, I wanted him to explain the reaction of the offenders. I detailed the disturbing incident and waited for some form of consolation.

"Oh yes, it's a lily-white neighborhood," he said making no apologies, except an apparent justification.

To know an opossum was to catch up with it in its natural habitat, and it was difficult for me not to see Rick as just another one of those ignoramuses, despite his exposure to my Caribbean culture. I played the hypocrite for another couple of days, since I didn't have a choice. And while Rick brushed the blunder under the carpet, I looked for the next exit to force his kind of hospitality in my rearview mirror.

By the time I called Sissy, Dawn was home and dry in Alaska, but I got the nod to take my place among a relatively friendlier set of people my own color on Nero Avenue. If according to Rick, he was living in a lily-white Wethersfield, I was about to be welcomed to a jet-black back-street in Bronx.

Veronica opened her door to me in her basement, which was not as fortified with furniture as that Connecticut mansion. However, I felt more stable in my element, thinking that if a problem arose, it would be something apart from skin-color.

Veronica seemed kind-hearted and told me to give her what I could to earn my keep. But all that would change when I was up on my luck. A short lady of about sixty, she held down two jobs that she attended one after the other every day. She perhaps didn't deserve to be tied down by a drunkard, but it was evident that that was how she straightened out her life, when she set foot in *The States*, somewhere in the nineteen seventies.

On the Sunday evening that I got to my new place, the weather was not so forgiving as the clouds spilled their guts. Although I had to strain my arms and twist my face to hurry out of the soaker, I still couldn't avoid noticing the conditions of the streets. Apart from the garbage bins that were put out at each gate to meet the Monday morning scavenger, the breeze blew wrappers along the sidewalk extending to the cul-de-sac, that was just below and behind the D-train terminal.

The track to Brooklyn was about to be engaged as hinted by the sound of the bell, which signaled that those who never made it should catch the next in line. A few blocks down, a mini park with monkey bars, swings and other playpen structures were available for fun time, under drier conditions. Mesh-metallic rubbish collectors chained to trees, kept their mouths open, hoping the waste papers and plastic bottles that were only inches from the transparent, hungry containers, would get up off their butts and get inside. There was a time and place for everything, and it was time for me to stand on my own two feet to get my own independence.

In that case, I had to do something to get my writing career up and running. But for the moment, I had to start with what I knew best, which was getting back in the classroom one way or another. The public library was my refuge to get my paperwork presentable, and my research reasonably reliable. The large brick building opened between 8 a.m. to 7 p.m., and it welcomed walk-ins from off the streets. Those included even the homeless, who often fell asleep, heads down on the tables, books, magazines or even newspapers listening to their woeful snores.

The facility was located on Gun Hill Road some blocks away from home. However, I had already proven that walking could be profitable when least expected. Hence, the daily exercise was definitely no problem. Unless, of course, I had to take cover from the occasional thunderstorms, that zigzagged life-threatening bolts of lightning down to earth out of the blue.

Just when I thought that prejudice was confined to one corner in Connecticut, I was unprepared to face the lesser of two evils. It came as a disguise in the form of the use of library computers that required a first-come-first-served administration. There was this eleven-o'clock confrontation, where a young female wanted to change things around to suit her position in the waiting area. I objected to her audacity, to get the typical African-American-woman-on-welfare to respect the patience of the people, who were there on time to see when she arrived. To my surprise she broke out into a brawl.

"You foreigner can't tell me what to do," she said. "Go back to your country." She obviously picked up my accent, which I found out later was a big issue to keep immigrants kenneled when they 'passed their place' with the average black American.

I knew that an attitude like hers was characteristic of the choke-chain syndrome found in places like the Cayman Islands, but I never understood it to be something I would have to look out for in the super-powerful USA. It was astonishing to me then, but I discovered later that black people were divisible by the least common factor, just like there was a deep fissure between them and the white folks.

The more I waited for my American dream to materialize, the more I became cautiously optimistic about the possibility of it becoming a reality. Especially when I also observed that a lot of the black population in the streets had battered self-confidence. They gave that impression by the kinds of music with which they identified, while walking around or riding bicycles with loud players in drug-infested regions. The Caribbean-Americans were more upbeat, and that seemed to arouse a kind of jealousy, which in turn appeared to provoke the kind of bitterness the lady in the library bottled up inside.

I was tired preparing for interviews to teach in high schools, just so that I could secure a professional permit along that route to make a smooth transition in status. Despite the two degrees plus twenty-five years of experience as notches up my belt, I only had one shot at seeing those principals, who by the way, happened to be all whites, even when the corresponding schools were located in a black neighborhood.

Then I decided to multiply my chances by seeking to enter the business of instructing English as a second language. The country was full of immigrants, documented and otherwise, who were from near and far, and needed the help of professionals with my kind of expertise. Of course, I had taught Shakespeare, Wordsworth, F. Scott Fitzgerald, name them, all over the world. And this would have been a grand opportunity to make my contribution in this métier. I responded to an ad, and a female fell for my phone call.

"I'm calling about the ESL vacancy advertised, to initiate my interest," I told her, and I prayed that the position was still available.

"Yes, we are seeking to fill the slot with someone who doesn't speak with an accent," she insulted.

"But everyone speaks with an accent," I pointed out. "People in Miami speak differently from those in New York, those in..." and I was about to string out a series of comparisons, before I was rudely interrupted.

"I am really not going to waste my time on the phone arguing with you about..." And it was my time to give her a dose of her own medicine.

"You're right! You can't because..." And she cut me off, just so she could have the last laugh.

I felt dejected and thought about throwing in my towel. Hence, I made arrangements to travel back to Jamaica at the start of September. According to the Air Jamaica travel agent, I could convert the ticket the first Friday to get on the Saturday flight.

On Thursday, August 30, 2001, I went to bed and dreamt that I was standing under a big tree staring at it. Then suddenly, the whole trunk of the giant split, and the ripped, woody section with limbs and leafy branches crashed to one side, next to me. I escaped without even a scratch. My heart pounded and I woke up feeling lucky. It was 4 a.m., and I knew that there was some significance attached to this fortune-telling phantasmagoria.

That morning I told Veronica that something was going to get in the way of my journey. But she thought I was talking gibberish while I revisited the reverie. Since it was my last day, I made myself useful, and my host took the timeout to accommodate my sendoff.

I was watching television in her living room at about eleven, when the telephone rang. Since nobody had ever called me on her line, I totally ignored the annoying ring in the interest of viewing *Jerry Springer*, my favorite program. Veronica took up the receiver, and after a greeting, she cast her eyes in my direction looking baffled. Then she handed the implement to me, a big question mark written all over her face. Her reaction had a domino effect, passing on the same perplexing paranoia to me.

"Hello, good afternoon, uh, uh, good morning!" I stuttered, getting the times confused. Meanwhile, I tentatively waited for the caller to say something that I could find out who knew me by that number.

"Hello, good morning." The male voice sounded calm, cool and collective. "Is this Bruce?"

"You're speaking to him."

The gentleman laughed to put my mind at ease, but I still didn't recognize him. When he figured that I was lost, he came clean.

"This is Moody," he revealed. "What are you doing on Monday? I spoke to my boss, like I promised, and he requested a rendezvous with you," he said, using his textbook-style expressions as usual.

Moody was *Mr. Perfect*, who never got tired of imitating the Queen's English, making endless errors in his efforts. I had completely forgot that we had run into each other in a Manhattan library one rainy day. I must have given him Veronica's information when he described his success in Paterson, where his director was an African-American operating a pre-school.

Married with two kids, Moody was trying to get his family to join him. On the day that we spoke in the city, he had taken his ten-year-old daughter on a tour, to give her a feel of what she was going to be a part of, soon and very soon.

The neatly dressed, miserly man seemed to be the kind who only helped when he stood to benefit. As he admitted, Nat had had a deadline from the authorities to field a full staff. Failing that, his contract would have been in jeopardy. God forbade if that happened, Moody's two-year search to achieve his American dream would have indubitably been put on hold.

When he told me about his employer's wish to have me in audience, I was supposed to be like the cow that jumped over the moon. However, I had become so depleted of the energy necessary to survive in those places, that many negative emotions, ranging from sadness to anger, attacked my constitution. I had to make a concerted attempt not to allow my intonation to transfer the inevitable feeling to my listener.

"I'll be in Jamaica," I told him, not knowing who to blame for my annoyance.

"Please postpone the flight because I already spoke on your behalf that you'd be there. You can't let me down now!" He was more determined than my zeal to stick around any longer.

"I'll see what can be done," I half-heartedly concluded, hanging up in a quandary.

Veronica couldn't believe her ears when she realized that my dream unfolded in the only conversation I ever had on her telephone, since living at her domain for the few weeks. On the other hand, I didn't know how to turn back the hands of time, to interrupt all the arrangements I had made to jump out of the frying pan into the fire. I finally swallowed my pride, if I could call it that, and decided to recoil my plans, to prepare to see the principal in Paterson.

I took the train to busy Manhattan, intending to locate Port Authority to catch the No. 161 *New Jersey Transit*. The day was warm and perfect for a full complement of pedestrians to bump and bore their way through crosswalks and sidewalks. Every so often, people's heads, shoulders and backs, feet hidden, herded along to create a wave of harnessed movement, confirming why those blocks welcomed the most visitors of all places.

I was a part of the viscous volume that floated along 42nd Street that Monday to get to my two o'clock appointment. I had to watch where I put my feet, while I was forced to slowly edge my way to avoid colliding with the head-on traffic. Simultaneously, I could not just stop too suddenly, lest the trailing crowd came crashing into me from behind.

While I was taking the necessary care to ensure everything went well down below, I had my next bewilderment from above. From the millions of us who crisscrossed paths along the quadrangles of high-rise buildings, a passing bird singled me out when its bowels acted up, just in time for my uncovered scalp. It was a refresher for my Gun Hill Road record, but this had a greater impact since I was dressed for a special occasion.

I did what I could to clean up the mess that spluttered over the short-sleeved, brown shirt that I wore. Luckily the marksman-like fowl must have eaten something of similar color, to make its waste blend with my top in perfect fashion.

I stepped onto the business-oriented piazza, squeezing myself between hotdog mongers and newsstand browsers, to wipe away the toxic fluid. When I finished and gathered my senses together, I stood for a while to let everything wear off. I raised my eyes spontaneously towards the sky, perhaps in light of the most recent incident, and the tallest buildings stared at me with superiority.

Billboards of all makes and models boasted their contents on high, to portray the city as the power of the people. I watched and wondered what would happen if those structures were to come tumbling down, trying to imagine what the town would do without them. In the end, I had to climb a skyscraping terminus dispatching buses to Paterson, and it was such a pleasure to find my way back to a low profile spot, which made me feel relaxed once again.

Nat was an obese guy in spectacles, whose tongue seemed to tie up with deceit, when giving the details of a job description. When the topic turned to money, it was made even more ludicrous. And after the few hours he commissioned me to stay for observation during school hours, I learned that everything he said was to be taken with a grain of salt. We discussed going to the attorneys, to get the paperwork in order for the work permit. However, I suspected that there was a long road before me. Worse still, I couldn't afford to change saddles in midstream.

I convinced myself that things were looking up a little, and I decided to move houses to be close to the school on Carol Street, a low-income community with Hispanics and blacks in majority. Not that these two ethnic groups seemed to have much in common, except when they met at the social welfare office to join a line, that curved from the inside of the building on to the main road. Other than that, one minority race occupied the east and the other the west, and both appeared to have a bone to pick with the next outsider who crossed the line.

The public library was just minutes away, but seconds from drug lairs that graduated addicts for the vertical Broadway, a main thoroughfare, which led straight to the town of Paterson. The school building, which was essentially a church convenience on a weekend, was centered in the basement of a brown, archaic, steeple-strong structure, and space, both inside and out, was indeed a luxury. Altogether, I wouldn't be missing Bronx, if the population and condition of the infrastructures in this unkempt common were the only indicators of change.

I returned to Veronica's lodge that Monday night, prepared to say goodbye to the hands that broke my fall. I went to bed about midnight after packing half of my stuff. I intended to get the other things together in the morning, before leaving for a rented place that Moody had premeditated for my purpose.

I dreamt that I was standing, not directly under but close enough to, a dead tree in Manhattan. A flock of multi-colored pigeons pecked at their feathers while perched way up on the dried, leafless branches. The sky above them was covered with cumulonimbus clouds, and now and again, the doves gave me a glance to confirm their comfort. Just then, the featherweight birds moved too hard, and upset the gigantic, buttressed carcass that could have vied for a place in the *Guinness Book of Record* during its lifetime. I watched as it came crashing to earth, while my limbs were too achy for me to even move a muscle. The skeleton disintegrated as the birds dispersed, and I awoke with my heart thumping like I had just finished the *New York Marathon*.

I was still lying in bed at about 9 a.m. on Tuesday September 11, 2001, reflecting on whether my mind was playing tricks on me. I suddenly decided to turn on the television that Veronica had put in my place for my plenitude. *Channel 11* was getting hot, showing airplanes charging into buildings, like paper replicas misdirected by urchins during class time.

At first, I spun it over in my head to think it might be a scene from a comedy, or perhaps someone was making a stupid joke. However, when the announcers got excited to report that everything was happening up to the minute, the story slowly straightened out, that the terrorists who had threatened to destroy the *Twin Towers* way in advance, had finally delivered on their promise.

I had to stay put at Veronica's for another week before I started school, and Nat was pleased to have me to save his skin. It was a different experience dealing with kids of the three-to-five age-range, but after the first month, I felt like I could stage my own show called *Big Daddy on Daytime TV*. My personality drew everybody's attention, from the coordinators at the corresponding workshops to those deployed as watchdogs by the regional superintendent of schools. Nat noticed all the accolades that I enjoyed, but for some strange reason, he kept putting off the legal portion that would let me fly high like an eagle. Instead, he often applied his tactics to get personal.

"What do you do on your weekends?" he asked one evening when he offered me a ride home.

I would have preferred if he had posed a different question. One requesting a date when I would be available for a trip to Gallagher, the lawyer Moody recommended to stitch up my story. I pretended not to have heard what Nat had on his mind, and he let me off without repeating himself. It felt like the boss had a hammer hanging over my head, and like he was intimating that I should play it safe by doing whatever he said, even if it were unrelated to the job.

I completed a term in that limbo, all the time Nat promising that we would make the journey to Manhattan to put in for the piece of paper. And like a delinquent dad who failed to deliver a toy at Christmas, Nat kept postponing each pledge as if it were another comfort for a desperate fool.

"When you come back from Jamaica, we'll go," he continued to play me, this time referring to my Christmas break to bail him out of his hypocrisy.

Coming back to the US two weeks after departure on a normal visiting visa, raised concerns at the customs. As a result, I got just two months to work with in my passport. Nat knew the position and promised that he would be prompt in respecting his responsibility.

Besides, he knew that both of us were liable to pernicious penalties, if we were caught in this labor misdealing. He had been paying me eleven hundred dollars in cash fortnightly, claiming to retain two hundred for the IRS, all of which was supposed to be on record. According to him, everything would be paid up, as soon as the legal aspects were resolved.

By the time we made it to Gallagher, I had received two payments since returning from Jamaica. The attorney's ninth floor office had mainly Indian employees answering telephones, and speaking to arriving clients through a small frontal window, directing them to sign a register and have a seat on the outside. The waiting space was full of Asians, interspersed with a few blacks and other disadvantaged and disoriented faces.

The atmosphere had a hopeless shadow cast all around, and from the telephone conversations between secretaries and clients audible through the little opening, I smelled deception. Not to mention the body language of the workers while they interacted in an air of uncertainty, as if to say they were interested in collecting cash, but after that any card could play.

Soon it was my time to come face to face with Gallagher in his chamber, and he had that mean look like Simon on *American Idol*. I sensed prejudice personified in this man, but because Nat was the one paying up front, I couldn't call the shots. Besides, I had waited so long, that half a loaf was better than none. Now that I managed to set foot in this legal office that had the White House appearance, I wasn't going to leave without having something to say at least we tried.

After I did my part, I even made some gruesome discovery that Nat had been grossly neglecting government regulations to underpay me all along. However, I was more focused on pointing out the time limit in my passport that was vital for Gallagher to act upon expeditiously.

"The 2nd of March is the expiry date," I told the lawyer, who immediately responded like I had just touched his last nerve.

"We are professionals here, and thanks but no thanks, we can do our job," he said, intimating I should mind my own business.

Although Gallagher was so testy when I reminded him about the deadline, I still referred to it while I was going through his door, just so that it would further make an imprint. He refused to take me on, but gave me a look of disdain, as if to say he could do without my money.

On the way back from New York, Nat again felt comfortable asking about my weekends, and I wanted him to get it in his thick head that it was none of his prerogatives.

"You know, the time is so cold. When I am not at work, I'm inside my four walls trying to stay warm." In other words, I meant that if he were trying to get me interested in having a drink with him as he twice recommended, that was just out of the question.

Two weeks later I followed up with a call to Gallagher, concerning submission of my documents to maintain my status. While he was not so arrogant this time, he assured me that though INS hadn't been contacted, he still had everything under control. I doubted every word he said, considering he sounded disorganized with his recollection. Moreover, his voice was far from convincing that he was on top of things. Meanwhile, back at school, the uncertainty affected the quality of my work, since I didn't know whether I was going or coming.

On March 3, 2002, I called Gallagher to get an update on the order of events. After answering a lot of quizzing from the secretary, plus holding the line for a long time, I suspected that something wasn't smooth.

"Mr. Welds, you need to visit my office. I think ... Please come to my office. We need to talk."

"What is it about?"

"You have to see me."

When I hung up the phone, I was not one bit surprised, and I began to think more about finding a way to get Gallagher to pay for whatever he did. With that in mind, I invested in a Dictaphone to meet my next-day appointment. Nat and I prepared to take our second trip to the sugar-tongued swindler.

When Gallagher saw us, his face turned red then pink, before he beckoned to the two seats facing his desk that were ours for the taking. Meanwhile, the secretaries moved about like little blind mice, fishing for files with guilt lingering on their faces. By that time, I had pressed the RECORD button while my secret gadget was still in my coat pocket.

"You have to go back to Jamaica," the heartless attorney began. "The date passed, and we didn't meet it."

I stared him in the eyes and told him a few words to his face.

"You got me in this predicament, and you are going to take me out of it," I retaliated in a calm manner, that perhaps stunned the hell out of him. I could tell that he was one of those, who stereotyped that black men were more predisposed to aggression than any other race. But now, he was willing to turn the table.

"What are you talking about? The freaking thing just got mixed up, and according to the law, you needed to have applied from your own country before you got here," he babbled elevating his voice, trying to sell me a story that I was supposed to buy, liked it or not.

I didn't say another single, solitary word. I reached in my pocket for the Dictaphone, and placed it on his desk immediately in front of me, all the time the red light blinked to show the device was actively engaged.

"Are, a, are, are you recording me?" he stammered, searching my face for clues that would suggest that this was only the beginning of the rolling mini-tape.

"Well, what do you think?" I answered to let Gallagher realize I was ahead of the game.

"A client is not supposed to tape his attorney without his permission," he intimidated, quoting the law like the devil to suit his own situation.

"That's why I am letting you know now. Better late than never."

Suddenly Gallagher knew his back was against the wall, and decided to clean up the mess that he created.

"I am going to submit your application and beg INS for leniency. This, in light of the World Trade Center disaster, since we are so close to the site."

"Now you're speaking my language." I gave him that look of admonition, to let him know that he was fooling himself with the wrong guy.

Meanwhile, Nat remained calm in one corner getting a good glimpse of what rating he needed to give me, and perhaps having a second opinion of the people he pooled from the Caribbean. However, at that point, I really didn't care about any impression I was making, as long as this cheat learnt his lesson the correct way.

Two months later, Gallagher called me with this I-told-you-so crack in his voice, to say that all was well that ended well. What was he trying to prove? Whatever! The most important thing was that he said he had received my H1B papers from INS, and that I should pick them up whenever. I didn't bother to get into any tongue-lashing tantrum with him, since I got what I wanted. And everything else was water under the bridge that I was set to cross if I wanted to continue any further.

CHAPTER SIX

My Social Security Saga

"Your permit is not in the system yet, so you just have to wait," said Hilary, the front desk clerk at the Federal Building in Manhattan, where I went and applied for my social security number.

Accessing that birthmark was the next bridge to build to get to my American dream. In *The States*, some people referred to this hallmark as the mark of the beast, likening it to clamping animals before freeing them into the wild. In other words, critics thought the ten-digit driver was more like a tracking device that lit up when the bearers do business. Meanwhile, wrongdoers chased this order of distinction like grave robbers on the hunt to exhume coffins cast in diamond.

"And how long will it take to find its way on your computer?" I asked, wondering what was taking the authorities so long, considering I had obtained my papers over a week.

"It normally takes six months, but don't call us, we'll call you."

Hilary hinted that this was just like another futile interview for the files. In actual fact, the second half of her response was for lack of a better way of saying that my chance of being taken to hell and back, would be greater than getting the number itself.

Why half a year, when both the Federal Building and the Social Security Office were like the president and the White House? These façades were like smoke and fire, and besides, computer efficiency in the USA was second to none in the western hemisphere. If I had tried beating the system in Jamaica hoping to get away with it at some US port, I would have been like a fugitive sniffing and selling cocaine at the front door of the Brooklyn 1st Precinct. Hence, it begged the question, why was a simple permit printed *by* a system not *in* the same system, with no final word available for a trying immigrant? That was about to be answered in the struggles to come, but I left the vertex of villainy feeling worst off than I entered, violated if anybody asked me.

So far so disillusioned, and I was disappointed that that might not have been the last of me that building actually had seen. Paranoia took control of my senses when I remembered that I would have to return to that prison-like facility, to find myself almost strip-searched like what I faced at the gate that nippy May afternoon.

In backtracking to that degrading nightmare, the sun was glowing but temperatures were in the mid-twenties to warrant wearing three layers on my back. *Homeland Security* demanded that I put my personal belongings on the x-ray conveyor machine. But when I crossed the line, the detector alerted the Hispanic and white boundary-guards that something was amiss.

I was told to step back and try again, further to which the men touched me from head to toe, like my picture was among those cornered in the *Twin Tower* tear-down. The hands of those ripped guys left no spot unspotted on my five-feet-nine-inches frame, trying to locate what was activating the cylindrical device.

Unless they were new on the job, something should have told them that my belt buckle was made of metal. But it didn't, until my face showed signs of succumbing to their harassment tactics. They told me to remove the article of clothing and the problem was solved. Then they looked pleased that they did a fine job of causing undue distress to someone outside their race, like they were simply following orders from up the ranks.

The good thing that came afterwards was the advice I got to use the office in Paterson for further investigation. This, in locating the 'lost' permit on which, getting my *Social* highly depended. Thank God I didn't have to sleep on a bus to drive fifty miles or more, only to be taken for a ride, with my sanity destroyed along with my pride. But that didn't mean the same sleeping sphinx wasn't lying in ambush wherever I tried. It was like a team effort tantamount to taking down a bull in the barnyard, and my next experience proved to be virtually the same as the first.

The Paterson Federal Building was set apart to overlook Market Street from behind and the extraordinarily congested Main Street in front. The revolving door revved up with the push of passersby, on their way in and out, on the day of my visit. Six months had not slipped by yet, but I figured that I could feign ignorance at worst if the clerk doubted my query for whatever reason.

"It's not ready," Cassidy, a Hispanic woman snapped after consulting her computer.

It appeared I had to watch every single thing that I did or said for fear that, if I even frowned or crumpled my brow for something I thought was not right, it was tacked to my record for future reprisal by the next consultant. One look at the monitor and Cassidy's composure was disturbed to drop my case like a hot potato, not wishing to touch it with a long stick. On that occasion, she won, but I left vowing to return with a vengeance.

I visited the office after the end of the six-month wait, and was greeted with an unexpected turn of events. It was one Friday in June when I felt a sudden gush of confidence that everything, including my dealing with the government, was going to work out right.

The morning started off with high temperatures, some humidity, but a great afternoon in the forecast. I went to work as usual, and used my lunch hour break to hurry downtown. The line was medium-length, and I breathed a sigh of relief that there was no need to wait too long.

My outfit consisted of T-shirt and jeans, not only to beat the heat, but also to minimize the level of harassment at the entrance, as I had definitely learnt from my experience. The patrons had obviously made up their minds to painstakingly go through the checkpoint, when in walked a white-bread visitor. He was a white male in jacket and tie, who skipped past the rest of us like we were just a waste of precious time. From the middle of the queue, I opened my mouth to let the three Hispanic security officers know that I still had blood running through my veins.

"What's up with that guy?"

"His buddy works here," Luke, the most robust replied. He blushed, which spoke for his cognizance that such nonchalance was simply defeating the purpose of the optimum security system, put in place since *Nine Eleven*.

I endured the favoritism smiling at the memory, that a mayor in Harlem got killed in his office when a so-called friend stepped past police, gun in hand, in like manner. At that time, it sparked outrage and the dead man's brother wanted to succeed him in office, wishing to salvage something from the whole serial-smitten incidents. My reflection went as far as picturing thousands that might suffer at the hands of the careless personnel in charge, when those let off the hook went on a rampage.

I just wanted to get in and get out as soon as convenient. When it was my turn, perhaps on account of opening my big mouth, the strapping fellow took it easy on me, even when my watch triggered off the metal detector at one go.

"Go," Luke said, and shifted his attention to the guy behind me. One 'good' turn certainly deserved another.

It was a welcome gesture, and I moved to the section that dealt with social security. There were signs showing areas that provided service for people changing status through marriage, naturalization and the whole kit and caboodle. Further down, a seated security officer gave out numbers to incoming seekers, and chairs were filled to capacity, emptying to be replaced by others waiting for a numbered window. I was waiting on the microphone caller to commission ticket no. 235, to go to the third station from the right of the doorway.

God answered my prayer and soon I was facing the adviser, while I had only fifteen minutes to spare to be back on the job.

"I'm Bruce Welds, and I am here to access my social security number. Here is my permit."

Missy was a different Hispanic, but I thought that even if she became familiar with my past, I should be out of the woods already, and it didn't matter if she huffed or puffed. She punched in the serial number at the far left corner of the document, tapped ENTER, and waited. She knitted her eyebrows and pursed her lips, while inspecting the monitor. Then she repeated the process, and again she must have come up dry.

"There's no application here for you," Missy said.

"I applied six months ago, and I was told to wait." I didn't know where to begin or what words to use to make sense with my story.

"Well, you'll have to apply again. There's nothing here for you."

That meant waiting another six months, without the rhyme or reason to follow up with even a letter to determine the headway of my effort. During that time a million and one sensitive issues could be spoiling. My enrollment to do the P3 certification in Education, tenable at William Paterson University and funded by the *Abbott Program*, was already suffering a major setback. By then, Nat would have collected over fifteen thousand dollars that I didn't think he was forking out to IRS for my future reclamation. I was cornered, and had come face to face with my obvious Waterloo.

I completed the form that Missy gave me, but couldn't wait to let her do the data entry. My patience must have been on reserves, for I started looking back to imagine where I would have been in Jamaica, if I had followed my heart before Moody changed it. Now it felt like I would have wasted my efforts having gone through so much, only to surrender to this snare, which I hoped was the last.

A fortnight later, I went through the same rigors to be in front of Missy again, only that she didn't recognize me the second time around. I couldn't blame her, since that office had thousands of applicants going in and out daily, with different sizes fish to fry. I gave her the necessaries, and she started to type in the basic information. Then she came to the more complicated parts that prodded her meticulousness.

"Is this your first application?"

"Yes," I confirmed.

Missy punched that in, but went silently contemplative when the computer must have rejected that response.

"Are you sure that this is your first? The computer is suggesting that you applied before."

"Ma'am, you don't remember me, but I remember you," I said, raising my voice so that the line of people paid attention to the gauntlet that I was about to throw down. "The last time I came to this office, you told me that there was no trace to show that my interest was represented in your machine. How come you are now saying the same thing that I said at that time?"

The obese woman looked me from the top of my head down to my chest, imagining the rest of my body below.

"Sir, I don't know what to say to you, but..."

"So what was the result of that application? I still need to know!"

"The computer is not showing anything, but you may need to apply again, and then take it up with the headquarters in Newark."

Newark was just like Paterson, and with the exception that the former had a regional airport to give it greater publicity, there was little to compare and contrast. The crime rate there made headlines on local television. And if a day passed without some black mother drowning the reporters with her sorrows, over the slaying of her street-bred son, then that war-torn community wouldn't be closing in on being the murder capital of New Jersey.

The streets were always congested with aimless or idle bystanders, and someone driving into town for the first time, quickly mistook it for Tenth Avenue in Paterson, where hustlers stare at strangers to peddle stuff ranging from marijuana to the best get-high drugs to date. Where were the cops when needed? For, if a pair of untrained eyes could pick up those miscreants, then undercover officers could sweep the streets. But if one took a closer look, the boys in blue could be right in the thick of it, messing with motorists to get these drivers to pay for illegal parking, or for even talking on a cellular phone behind the wheel. Talking about prioritizing!

So this was the place to which Missy recommended that I took my grouse. And it was like I wasn't supposed to feel threatened by the very existence of ulterior eventualities that could bring an end to my pursuit of happiness - please! It took me a lot of psyching-up and second thoughts, to get me going to such predictable branch of the borough, but I finally found the Federal Building. However, it was not before the search produced a drama of its own.

I arrived at the center, swarmed by solicitors that reminded me of a typical Oxford Road gathering, where drowsy eyes kept hope to stay awake. It was ten o'clock in the morning, but there was a line that had already roped its length, from the closed door of the building to cover three blocks of busy street sidewalks.

Some early risers took their seats on the square concrete slabs fixed in the ground, while some stood with their arms folded. Others peered forward every now and then to see when the workers arrived to open the doors. One could have only imagined that the employees, who entered the four-story construction to lock themselves in with one turn of a key, were still turning in bed when the person at the front of the queue had taken up position.

The morning sun was changing its heat gradually, and a few umbrellas started to launch open. Sweat was also making its marks along the necks and clavicles of those in low-cut shirts and blouses. Then a guide began to collect documents belonging to one group, a little before another personnel announced a call for a different set. This, to give a kick-start to speed up the process by the time the patient people made their way into the building.

After that, the marshals sent the people in ten at a time, using discretion when to let consecutive groups in past the post. After checking the whole proceedings, I surmised I was perhaps in the thirtieth batch getting ready to bail out of the broiling sun. That was far from having any cooling influence on my brain, but I felt like I had to stick it out for a worthy cause.

I labored in the heat to boil down to being in the fifth set from the front. Suddenly a man, dressed differently from those directing traffic, appeared from out of nowhere, speaking with the highest level of authority.

"We only have time for three more groups. The rest will need to come back another day," he said, walking along the full stretch of over a thousand sun-burnt, weary waiters to repeat his message.

I felt like collapsing, once the blatant heartlessness was pushing me over the edge. So far, I was barely hanging on to make the grade. But since my reason for enduring had been knocked to the ground, I was more vulnerable to the next available excuse to throw my hands in the air. The crowd hesitated as if to listen for some rebuttal, or for someone to say the messenger was not to be taken at his word. But apparently, the judge's decision was final.

That night I slept like a log, not being in the frame of mind to even plan another date to make it back to Newark. After giving it another thought, I came to the conclusion, that staying overnight in a motel might be the best bet to get in that line, ahead of the accustomed crowd. However, I decided to leave the idea where I found it, and stuck to waking up with the rooster, to reach the public hotspot on time for the waiting game.

It was 1 a.m. on Monday of the following week, eight days to the date that life threw another curved ball, aimed at my head in that Newark scuffle. I was like a hitchhiker on Broadway in Paterson, trying to flag down the next taxi to get to the bus station downtown. At that hour, cab drivers were quick converts to skeptics, when looking out for strayed and stranded customers. And they had a point in their reluctance, since that was when drug users and abusers came out like skunks to claim their turfs, and everybody, including the lawmen, had to get used to that switch of land use.

At the bus park, the silent street was like a cemetery, and the only ghosts around numbered about ten homeless sleepers, huddled with their faces hidden between their palms, or covered by some blackened, dirt-pasted pieces of clothing. They seemed assured by an ostrich that they were as safe as they could get, as long as their heads were not in the open air to give away their identity.

A bus slowly drew in the terminus, but the destination bar didn't do me any good with its unlit showcase. It sidestepped all the available slots, to stop directly in front of the terrace of the refreshment shop that entertained commuters during the day. The vehicle throttled for some five minutes, while the black driver kept the doors closed, ignoring my quizzical stare to figure out where he was bound. He yawned and shuffled, exhibiting signs of disbelief that anybody in his right mind could ever be on the road at that hour, much less looking to get on an empty, fifty-seat bus. As sure as the changes that took place day and night, a customer was usually assured that he was always right. But pathetically not when I was viewed in this dim light, from a tired busman's misguided insight.

At about 1:45, he raised his hand to roll down the destination plate, before the entrance door retracted open. It was indeed going to Newark and what a relief! I hopped up on the steps, and took out a ten-dollar bill from my wallet to pay my passage. I handed it to the weary conductor, but instead of taking it, he looked at me as if I were from another planet. I kept my hand stretched forward with the money, searching for some kindness in the face of this retiree-reminiscent figure. But he shook his head disobligingly.

"You need the correct change," he said, pointing to a small chute beside the steering wheel, specifically for the purpose of accepting bucks and quarters.

The machine was never made to give change to commuters, so the correct amount was necessary at all times. The once-in-a-while voyager wouldn't know or remember that bit of information, and a seasoned bus operator would be tempted to think that that sort of common knowledge should be at the fingertips of the normal public.

"What's the fare?" I asked, hoping I could force my fingers into the small waist pockets of the denim pants that I wore, to come up with the required amount.

"It's two sixty-five."

This guy's tongue was too skew with words, and I was beginning to see difficulty in the making.

"Can you break this up from your personal stash?" I implored, still pointing the bill in his direction, and still standing on the steps of the idling vehicle.

"No." And he motioned me to make up my mind, either to put the ten dollars in the acceptor, or step back and get my acts together.

Just when all hope was fading, and I was being overcome with the idea that I might have to wait for another hour to catch the next bus, by which time I would have been hopefully better prepared, a second guest appeared. He was a white man in his late thirties, carrying a backpack and appearing to have missed the last transport the night before. When he heard of my situation, he was quick to lend a hand.

"Here!" offered Johnny-come-lately, giving me three dollars, and stating that that was the best he could do at that moment.

"On the way, hopefully someone coming on, might be able to split this ten, so you can get yours back," I mentioned, feeling guilty of causing inconvenience for the good guy.

"That's okay. Leave it at that. This is your lucky day," said my Good Samaritan.

It was already four when I got to Newark and specifically at Columbus Avenue, where the line was already half of what I had joined on my first adventure. It was the same thing all over again; men appearing during the parching heat to procure the cut-off point, only that this time, I found myself on the inside. By the time I made it through the door, to face this Aussie-white, female representative, it was already noon. She perhaps thought I was her everyday-client, but she couldn't have been more mistaking.

"This is my work permit, and I had applied for a number and waited according to instructions. However, after six months, nothing happened and I'm here to make sure an unfair game doesn't play twice."

I hoped I was making sense, but it was so difficult to imagine that, when it was so easy to assume the listener was right there in my mind to follow every little incident that was not so simple to put in words. Angela was this woman over the counter, and she looked tentative as if she got the hint that she might have to do something quick to duck from this challenge.

"Let me see what we have here," she began, taking enough time to think up what she could, to exonerate her organization from any plain blame. She punched in the number found on my document, glancing at the nearer corner of the greenish computer sheet that she held between her forefingers. Then she read the information on the monitor with a defensive demeanor, hoping to counteract anything that featured in my favor. "Go upstairs and get the officials there to honor their decision," Angela advised straight-faced.

"What do I tell them? Shouldn't you give me some note to indicate that I got directives from your authority?" I tried everything to be logical in my communication.

"Just tell them that we sent you."

"What's your full name?"

"Can't tell you that."

And she looked to press the light button for the next customer. Though I felt stupid while I was about to do something that lacked substance of sobriety, I walked away without a choice, other than to follow some silly order. I took the elevator to the third floor, where the Social Security Office was in full swing. There were many complainants in the waiting area, and security officers stood on guard duty.

I was losing my patience, and was poised to explode with the prick of a prickle. I took a number and waited anxiously to hear it on time. Then it finally happened, and I looked Sonia in the eye through the separating, transparent, glass partition to relate a story that had become a botch and an annoyance to repeat.

After listening with intermittent interruptions from the rep immediately across from her, Sonia, still perched on her high stool, told me to have a seat and wait. I must have endured an hour before she called me back to her side of the counter. I rushed to her window with renewed spring in my steps.

"What's your grouse again?" she trivially asked, with absolutely no respect for my time and humanity.

I was gobsmacked by Sonia's insensitivity, and didn't know where to start with this mind-erosive, conflict-tolerance tale. It would have been different if she had indicated some familiarity with say, half of the horrifying conundrum. Perhaps it would have been more encouraging to fill in the missing pieces. However, repeating the whole thing felt like I was about to lift up an elephant all by myself. I prepared for the torture, before providing the details of my delusion. Again, she listened with a divided attention, typing on her keyboard like she perfected the art of multitasking. When she figured I was finished, she gave me another little bit of her charity.

"Have a seat again. I'll get someone to deal with your case," said Sonia, after which, she disappeared in a backroom, leaving me with the impression that her twenty-minute absence was taken to talk things over with someone higher in authority.

I waited another forty minutes, by which time, Sonia had returned and was in active conversation with about three other female co-workers within the *Employees-Only* area. Meanwhile, the customer lobby recurrently packed up with people, passionate to know about their prerogatives. Suddenly her eyes caught mine, as I sat looking like a puppy in distress, and she beckoned to me to come forward. I could tell that my call was a by-the-way commission, and she might need some reminder to get moving on my wavelength.

"What's your..." Sonia suddenly realized that I would confirm she was tripping, if she were to have asked me to repeat myself one more time. "Ah mm, Lorenzo, Lorenzo, deal with..." And she turned to me, while a Hispanic male who was on his way to the back, stopped on demand. "What's your name again?"

"Bruce Welds," I said.

"Deal with Mr. Welds," she instructed, in a way that it was confusing to know which of them was the superior.

Lorenzo twisted his body sideways between the gals in the left corner, to lean his ear towards a crack where he could hear me. If he only knew how much I felt like I was imposing on someone who had 'better' things to do with his time! I had to tell the tale from scratch, and I sensed he had a prepared response on the tip of his tongue.

"We can't help you, because if we do, it would be unfair to everyone else," Lorenzo said, without giving my situation any serious consideration.

"I am not asking for any concession." I started to raise my voice. "If you were listening to me any at all, you would have known that I applied first and you bumped off my…"

"No shouting!" a security guard intervened.

"Nobody is going to tell me how to talk. Enough is enough." I turned my attention to address the black, robust uniform-stricken personnel, slinging a gun on either side of his waist.

"You may feel you have a point," the sub-officer toned down somewhat, "but there's always an alternative to a boisterous behavior," he said.

"Well, you just have to put your foot in my shoe," I retorted.

Then I continued the uproar, like it was the only recourse I knew to give me the justice that I deserved. The guard stepped a little closer.

"I will have no other choice than to put you out, if you continue like this," he said.

"What difference would that make?" I asked with that look of anger. "I wouldn't lose anything apart from the memory of brutish faces like yours!"

Just then Lorenzo perhaps figured that I had pertinent reasons to be mad, and he called me to share his invasive space in the corner.

"The best that I could do for you, is to issue a stamped evidence to indicate that you visited our office, and we could take it from there," Lorenzo offered.

Anything was better than nothing, and I calmed down to listen. My silence meant consent, and he did what he proposed. After accepting the paper, I ran downstairs instead of waiting in the carpeted corridor, to ride the spacious lift. It was exactly 4:30, and the guard stood at the door of the Federal Office, waiting to turn the key to let out the final two clients, who were being individually assisted.

I waved the piece of paper that I received upstairs, to see if the doorman would give me some form of special treatment. However, he whispered 'closed' to me, and I got the message. Drained and confused, I left unfulfilled to catch the bus back to Paterson. I gave up.

Two weeks later, a letter arrived in the mail. When I opened it, the content was a small, blue, rectangular paper, marked with the numerals 1-311-740… which was what the fuss was all about. I had the document in my hand but didn't know what to do with it. I was like the guy who literally burned the midnight oil to cram for an exam, and fell asleep ten minutes after beginning a two-hour paper the next day. Better yet, I felt like I was Nelson Mandela, who fought to put an end to apartheid, and when freedom finally hit him in his face, there was not a damn thing he could do with it.

Meanwhile, Nat had woven an entangled web for himself, winding up on Schindler's list to lose his contract. I saw everything coming like I was Elijah the prophet. It started with months of misuse of funds, after collecting fifteen grand in government grant for each student annually. With a population of close to a hundred, one simply had to do the math to unearth the cheater's wealth. He just couldn't keep his fingers out of the kitty.

"Let's go to the bank," Nat said. "I am going to draw a check of ten grand in your name, like it's your accumulated salary," he plotted. "Then when you cash it, pass it over to me."

I looked apprehensively at him, but he tried to play it down as if he were in control of his gargantuan game.

"Are you sure it's okay?" I asked, knowing fully well that something was just not right. I worked in a bank during my younger years, but Nat perhaps hadn't had the time to revise my résumé. What a shame!

"You're okay! Just don't show any signs of incertitude," he reassured. "My father used to operate a *McDonald's* food store before he died. After his passing, I ran the restaurant, so I know about business here in the USA."

God might have rested his dad's soul, but we went to *Chase* and withdrew the money as planned. That kind of activity became commonplace down the line, so that cash flowed generously into the gold digger's mine. Meanwhile the already shabby classrooms underwent rapid deterioration to attract the attention of the weekly watchdogs.

Then Nat was slashed from the *Abbot Program*, based on information reaching his superiors. As expected, an auditing report detected that he had cooked the books. He had to make half of his staff redundant without redress, while he appealed the above irretrievable decision. He coldheartedly told me to stay home and wait for his revival. How was I supposed to stand the test of time, when he wasn't going to pay me a single dime?

Now that I got the number, the absence of which according to Nat, had tied his hands, disabling him from submitting my tax, I thought I was ready to set him free to do things in my favor.

"I had been using the number on the permit to pay your taxes," he said, after I introduced my social security information to him. "I only found out that that was possible a few months ago," he continued.

I meant to ask him about the figure he fed to IRS, but I recanted. In spite of his crooked conduct, it felt pretty awkward doubting the integrity of someone who was in charge of an institution responsible for shaping young minds. However, when the *W2 Form* arrived in my mailbox, the income tax collector only received three out the total fifteen thousand that Nat deducted for over two years.

I didn't say anything to the big, fat wolf. But his conscience had him on the edge of his seat, causing him to keep threatening to cancel my permit, hoping that I would leave my American dream to leave him in peace.

Well, what more could I say? Many people had had varying fates, and since I couldn't keep my mouth shut, I happen to run into a few while comparing notes. Believe me, the half had never yet been told.

CHAPTER SEVEN

Comparing Notes

"The IRS needs to go after him for cheating me out of my tax returns," I told Knox, a man in his fifties who I met at Eastside Park in Paterson.

"Only if you report him. You don't give a sucker like that a second chance," Knox advised, "for he could easily become your meal ticket to that American dream."

It was one of those mayflower-spring mornings, when I felt depressed and took a stroll to steer clear of dull fear. I was pretty much doing some exercises to maintain my health at the time that I ran into this man. He looked young and skinny enough to attract any woman in need of a match, though his movement sent an entirely different message. It seemed he was out to get some early sun from sitting on a concrete bench, comfortably designed to surround a statue of some white man, who was believed to have become a hero after his death.

The solar rays weren't enough to prevent too much of the chill, but nature's heating system was already where it reflected us as a standing duo, our shadows shifting with all of our body movements, on the breast-high encircling walls. Nightingales chirped their multiple songs in the interim, pecking at the tiny, red, wild fruits that decorated between the pin-shaped leaves on two trees, purposefully planted to face each other on either side of the surrounding mural enclosure.

The large, square tiles below picked up the pieces of leftovers that fell from the beaks of these birds, or the floor was stained by the spluttered, easily-bruised, juicy round fruits that were overripe and fell at the jerk of the branches. Dog walkers and fitness freaks cut their concentration, and took a glance over the secluded area to see that two heads were on top of two pairs of shoulders. But the rest left something for the busy trekkers' imaginations.

I was the one to initiate the conversation, suspecting that Knox was a countryman. When he realized we either had something in common, or were two polar people, he shuffled to get up using his walking stick that was lying low, then let his adrenalin flow with the excitement from the experience that I minced up to suit the time and place. He scrambled around the tourist-attractive, makeshift, open-air center that usually sustained the padded bodies of homeless men napping off their night's lodging. Only the musty smell of urine and the toxic sight of empty beer cans in brown paper bags, used to evade cops' scrutiny, gave away the surrounding as that belonging to a black neighborhood.

Knox entertained my company, joking about his American dream, while taking different puffs of what at first resembled cigars. However, when the scent went up in smoke, it was marijuana that was making his day. I told him I was into education, and he planned to solicit my service as a private tutor, to give some meaning to his life that had come to a standstill after a major accident.

"Sorry about the smoking," he corrected himself, after remembering that my profession might not have the tolerance for such practice.

"Don't worry, I have learnt to survive in America," I said to calm him down.

Knox knew he never had a thing to worry about, and was perhaps the happiest man alive, despite only just having gone under the knife business-wise, to secure the millions that should be piling up in his bank account any minute while we spoke. And also, in spite of his family, that had been insensibly dismantled only moments too soon, as a result of his now ex-wife's shortsightedness and disobedience.

"Look," he pointed at his new 2004 Ford Expedition. "Do you see that handicap sign in the front? That's just one of the fringe benefits."

I focused my eyes keenly to see the little blue instruction slip dangling from the front part of the roof of the bluish-gray truck, and it brought back a disgusting memory of this seventy-year-old woman, Velma. She was a wretched Jamaican neighbor of mine, who used a similar ploy to get preferential treatment from the government, after her husband, for whom it was originally and legitimately intended, had long passed.

Okay, that might have been a partial fulfillment of *her* American dream, but she used the personalized parking at her gate to be a spur in each of her neighbors' side. She often kept the special spot empty, parking her jalopy way below or above the tow-away zone, and if anyone dared putting his motor just an inch too close to the vacant space, she made sure the police promptly paid him a visit. And as for the invasive vehicle, the pound picked it up.

Since Nat had put my life on hold indefinitely, I bought a 1997 Ford Expedition to ease the pain in finding a job out of town, though I was bound by residency restrictions. Fourteenth Avenue wasn't far from Carol Street, so my feet were my carriage during the time I worked with Nat. Now that Garfield got my attention, an SUV was the solution to even the snowy seasons.

"Somebody bought a new truck around here," said Velma to Joyce, the owner of the house where I lived. The latter was a private woman, and suspected that the monster wanted to poke her nose into what really never concerned others. Least of all someone with whom, the listener knew, I had never exchanged words. Joyce ignored the comment, until the satanic sorcerer felt compelled to spell things out. "Is it belonging to the man living in your house?" she pried, in as much as she didn't even know my name.

"Yes."

"That's a pretty expensive truck for a person living under someone's roof," replied the rambunctious Jezebel.

Not that I was too surprised by Velma's comment when it finally reached my ears. The wrinkles on her face said exactly the kind of devil that possessed her mind. Apart from having a creepy kind of composure, like a green lizard camouflaging undercover to get a dim view of people in progress, she had the demeanor of the black widow spider, destined to be without a husband for the rest of her miserable existence. Everybody perhaps knew that it was the ghosts of people like Velma that lived in haunted houses. And so, with the little life that was left in her, she obviously planned to make mine a living hell.

Be that as it might, months passed and people either loved the brown eye-catcher that faithfully carried me around, or they didn't, depending on whether they had a good heart. Mysterious scratches appeared on the panels every now and then, but that didn't stop it from standing out on the road, especially when it was parked behind Velma's old, green Cherokee.

One early morning, I woke up and peered through my window from the upper floor of the red, one-family house I shared with Joyce. My vehicle was missing. I always parked immediately in front of our building over the other side of the road. But occasionally when Velma made her side a clean sweep, that provoked stress to find a convenient place, and I was forced to leave my truck on an adjacent road near enough to Barnet's Hospital.

That Friday, I was just out of bed, so I rubbed my eyes to get a clearer vision, hoping desperately that I was mistaking. It was some time in August and the trees along the avenue were in full bloom. The green leafy vegetation from the acorn-bearing overgrowths, stood pat up to my double-glazed window, while countless squirrels felt at home chasing each other along intrusive power lines before scampering across the underlying branches.

When the bushy tails of the petite rodents couldn't balance their leaping feet, they flew across the obstacles like they belonged to the Amazon rainforest. When such activities blocked my view, I ran downstairs hoping that I had lost my memory overnight, and that the truck would appear out of somewhere to quickly come to my rescue and end my nightmare.

I dragged the front door open, but nothing changed, although I could now see all the usual spots where I would normally have left my motor. A hospital janitor was cleaning the fenced-off employees' parking lot on the far side, and apart from his presence, the morning was as calm as the eye of a storm.

"Have you seen my truck?" I asked breathlessly, interrupting the sweeping strokes of a man I always saw, but had never found it pleasant in my heart to greet with any degree of compliment.

He took a moment of his time and penetrated my appearance with inquisitive eyes, as if to wonder why I was wearing only pajamas, or if he might need to get me some psychiatric help in an instant.

"If it's a brown Expedition, the cops took it," he said. "I was wondering why they were towing it, but you never know. Or maybe you have an enemy."

Velma had struck again, this time from an unexpected angle. I didn't believe that my own countrywoman would have stooped so low to stand in my way, but I lived to confirm that crooked people carried the look in their faces. The Wednesday before the towing, I had parked the eye-burner behind Velma's space, and it was then she noticed that the registration had expired according to the yellow sticker in the left hand corner of my windshield. Now, even the blond-haired taxi driver, who took me to the pound to sign for the release, knew it was a setup.

"The cops don't come to tow unless someone summons them," he said. "It's a shame because they might only seize your car if they discovered the delinquency during a spot-check."

"I know who did it," I said.

The long-bearded, hairy-faced cabman didn't have to give any more hints. Velma was the only neighborhood watch, who threatened to call the city officials for something as simple as when the Mexicans living two gates down, piled up pieces of board at the side of their house. She saw it as an eyesore, and thought that the best she could do was to hide her stick to hit the pits.

That was a long story that just flashed through my mind like a thunderbolt, and I was still listening to Knox when David pulled up behind our trucks.

The two SUV transports were docked along a little island, which was well maintained with green grass around a fountain. David had recognized both license plates, and had decided to stop and finish the cup of *Dunkin Doughnut* coffee that he was sipping along the way.

I had met him the same way I became acquainted with Knox, and it was this meeting that gave me the understanding that both originated from Clarendon in Jamaica. I might have had my own journey packed with interesting moments, but both those guys were not only more mature in terms of age, but were also more street-smart in playing the system. I had a good idea of David's dilemma, but when those two compared notes, I never needed a classroom.

"What happened to you?" asked David, obviously surprised to see that Knox had suddenly seemed to become a part of the disabled community.

I took that to mean that they both hadn't seen each other in years, understandable based on David's downfall, which made this gray-haired guy forget that the world was still turning. David ended a relationship with one girl, got married to another, and after years of devotion to his family, he thought the fire was beyond rekindling between him and his ex. He started a restaurant, and since he had applied to the government for bankruptcy, he and his ex agreed to become business partners, so that he could put her name in front, with the underhanded understanding that they both shared the ownership.

David, then in his forties, must have been drunk when they arrived at that decision, not anticipating that the deceiver would have held him at ransom, when he failed to fuel an affair at her fancy. He should have known that play, not to have fallen for it, yet he still didn't get it when she turned the blade of the knife for him to have and to hold.

"I had an accident," Knox said, but instead of looking downcast, he wore a smile while hopping around, showing a kind of physical discomfort that had escaped my notice before David's arrival.

A version ran across my mind spontaneously. I had seen sorry cases on television where people applied for disability, but were caught lifting loads that able-bodied men couldn't attempt in dreams. I didn't know about the knack until I saw it with my own two eyes in New Rochelle. A cab carrying three passengers collided with a private car that was driving in the wrong direction.

The Caribbean club that I attended that Saturday night, had just regurgitated its visitors into the streets, and I was waiting for my company to get on our way. It wasn't such a hard hit, but the accident startled me, especially when I noticed that while the two vehicles locked headlights, the passengers sat still like statues. The offending driver jumped out and got busy, since it was clear who was in the wrong. I was very concerned that the motionless two ladies and a guy might have been injured, since they appeared to have been speechless. However, their eyes were wide open.

"Why don't they try to get out?" I asked. "What are they waiting for?"

"No, they can't! They'll lose the thousands they stand to collect from insurance," a man from the crowd corrected, taking some of his precious time to educate me.

I watched while I heard the sirens of ambulances and cop cars flare up, flooding the scene to give paramedics the range to lift the 'patients' out of the cab. The emergency guys took extreme care in handling the fakers to circumvent lawsuits, and then they placed the helpless cheats on the waiting stretchers. The busy team of medical experts bluffed their way through the streets with the sound of excitement, heading for the nearest medical center.

That tactic reminded me of two Spanish girls who studied English in my class. Agnes and Liz became enemies for a peculiar reason, laced with insurance greed in a similar situation. Agnes gave Liz a lift to school when the road was too covered with snow. When they got to the stoplight on Riverside Drive, another car coming from the opposite direction couldn't hold its brakes, and Agnes went crashing into a lamppost to save both drivers from a head-on collision.

The car never had much damage, but Liz claimed she had head injuries and decided to press charges against her host's insurance company.

"Even now one side of my head feels like there is no sensitivity," Liz explained, with that usual Spanish accent, trying to justify the fake operation that she and her physician had fabricated. "I have two more times to be under that anesthesia," she told me when we met the first day of the second semester. She could hardly speak my language but she knew how to project herself as the victim.

However, Agnes had a different vision of the woman she was simply assisting that weather-beaten morning.

"That's a wicked girl," Agnes said in the equivalent of the best English expressions that she could muster. "I didn't have to take her in my car, but now she wants to get money at my expense."

And the last part of her sentence was the living truth, given that when an insurance company paid for any liability, the premium of the perpetrator tripled if not quadrupled consequently. It was quite unusual to see two Spanish people in such a fight, considering they were the clannish type that nothing could divide. But when it came to collecting a tidy sum like thirty thousand dollars, these two were willing to cast their similarities aside and put asunder their foolish pride. Which was what Liz did before disappearing to enjoy her spoils in peace.

"I had an accident too," David weighed in, to say that they had both had it up to their throats. "I have only been out of the hospital three weeks now, and I am slated to go back to follow my doctor's orders," he said, using his left hand to help the right to raise it above his head. "See, right now I can't even use one of my arms."

David was rehearsing how to bear the name and play the game right there in front of us, considering that this front was to become his second nature. He couldn't afford to be another living, statistical proof, caught doing a Herculean task after declaring disability. Apparently, there was no shortage of finding public officials as accomplices to that kind of crime, and doctors and even judges seemed to bulge their eyes when rippers appropriate their opportunities.

"Do whatever he tells you," Knox coached his pal, and the former had our attention one hundred percent when he gloated about the power-ball behind his victory.

It was obvious who was on the upper rung when Knox did his dance of the millions. And as he described, even the high court judge that handled his divorce wished he could jig at the subject's rags-to-riches party. Speaking about parties, the festivity began when Knox was all about business, trying to make ends meet, using his menial jobs that he juggled on a daily basis. It was a bright and sunny lunchtime in summer, hence the reason he bought two chicken patties and a can of soda, to gulp down at the slightest chance.

On reaching Park Avenue, a *Daily News* truck running a stop sign, ploughed into the driver-side of his work vehicle, pinning him to the dashboard, where he sustained injuries to his spine, legs and other fragile places on his body.

"*Daily News*! That's a gold mine you're talking about! You're lucky!" David looked at his compatriot with envy in his eyes. "I wish I were in your skin right now," he said.

"That's what they all say," Knox chuckled. "You should see the judge who handled my divorce! When he heard '*Daily News*', he looked at me with this you-lucky-bastard blush in his black face. I could tell he wanted to give me his wig to take my position."

"So why were you getting a divorce at such a 'pleasantly' dramatic time in your life?" I asked, while David backed me up with my bonus question.

"Because that woman of my four kids was stupid. She had an affair. Yet, I wasn't the one who filed. But she followed foolish tutors and lost," Knox expounded.

"And she could have collected millions for herself, not counting your portion," David analyzed. "All she needed to have done was to claim spousal disability and the world would have been hers, stupid!"

"That's women in America, they follow friends to screw their husbands," Knox whined, showing that his emotions were still aching from the split.

"Nonsense!" I remarked. "The ordinary American woman would have put off that divorce until she became rich to make the switch."

"The judge put off the case four times to get her to reconsider, and even so the dimwit didn't read between the lines. He told us to see how best we could make up, but she insisted to have it," explained Knox, and I could tell he was disappointed.

"So what about the children, wasn't she thinking about them?" I just couldn't see past the stupidity.

"Apparently not," Knox reiterated. "It was only after the judge regrettably granted the decree, she realized her mistake, and looked at me as if she wanted to share my fortune. But that was out of her hands."

"Your life is set. That's your American dream. Some people find it, others take a lifetime," David deduced. "Mine might not be as good as yours, but it's something to start me off. I have another operation in a few weeks."

"Just do it!" Knox encouraged.

In my book, Knox had to share the blame for the whole imbecility. And I had to assume the O J Simpson *if-I-did-it* hypothesis to internalize why I also held him accountable. The nouveau-rich and his woman were just like the average love-is-blind pair that pointed fingers at each other when things went wrong, rather than remembering the kids in the midst, to look out for their interests. If I had found myself with Knox's keys, and my stubborn wife couldn't see the forest for the trees, I would have put aside all differences, and explain to her that a timely reconciliation was important to shake the money tree, so that our children could pick up the greens. After we shook it like an earthquake, the kids would get everything that was at stake. Eventually, even if we were still at war, life for them would be different by far.

But no, they had to be typical! Once they were breaking up, each wanted the worst calamity to befall the enemy they made of one another. Therefore, even if Knox saw the infidel about to fall in a pit, he wouldn't have remembered that she was still the one to whom his beloved children had that instinctive attachment.

Just when the three of us thought we were out of harm's reach, enjoying the good catch that took two by surprise, a cop car shadowing us, slowly came to a halt on the peripheral road across from where we stood. There was a canopy of big trees along that drive, where older folks cozily treasured the loneliness of their lives in massive mansions that never seemed to welcome kids. The white car, with red and blue streaks, stealthily appeared at an awkward fork in the road, where the lone officer could make a right to be on the one-way turn, which led to the baseball field below the hill on which we converged. Or, he could make a left that would take him the other way that joggers chose.

We couldn't tell a police officer what to do. But when one singled out three black men just to spy on them without adequate justification, it felt uncomfortable like what was deemed racial profiling. There he was, a white man sitting around the wheel, and pretending to be doing some paperwork.

"Get the hell away from here," I backhandedly flashed my right arm at him, to assert our disapproval of his presence.

After I repeated the gesture in his face, the idle lawman drove off and honked his horn, as if to say I owed him one. An officer could easily get even with a motorist, especially when both shared the same streets, alleys and community. I knew that, but I was fed up with all the injustice that I had heard happening all around.

All three of us decided to break the circle for the simple reason that chaos usually started with a hole in the dam, and before long, tragedy struck in New Orleans to upset the unforgettable scenes. After referring to a few cases of police pressuring black men in separate incidents, we radiated in different directions, leaving me to do my usual reflections.

My radio was on, as I cruised along Park Avenue, where convenient stores owned or operated by immigrants from the Dominican Republic, opened their doors to the minority population. The news was still current with the Sean Bell shooting case, and the cops involved in using fifty-odd shots to bring down the unarmed black man, stood on solid grounds. Though the killers were principally blacks, analysts contended that those officers were tokens of the order, which upheld veiled rules rallying against equal rights.

I really didn't attach my tentacles to any one particular side, assuming that dead-bury-their-dead attitude, to distance myself as a 'foreigner' from the contaminants in the air. If I had found myself in any difficulty, I couldn't have looked to even my own countryman for any form of help, hence, I had to take things personal. Plus, there were double standards involved, where rappers degraded the black population, yet expected respect to start from the outside in, rather than vice versa.

I didn't possess the time or patience to cut my mission to entertain semantics. I arrived in the USA to see black people with issues, and after a time, it became evident that I would have to take what was mine and resign, lest I lost my life. Or, end up behind bars where black men's place had been reserved and preserved. I knew it was best to avoid certain places, and limit frequent contacts with some groups, though it appeared certain that every dog had its day.

My day came while driving on Park Avenue to use Route 20 to get to work 8:30 one morning. Park Avenue left all its madness and mayhem behind after its intersection with 33rd Street, where a stoplight slowed things down. Then the residential area stood out with a few Jews and their synagogues initiating a noiseless community. The men in black trudged the sidewalks wearing felt hats, detouring three blocks further on to enjoy the scenery of the public park, before using the side roads to go around in circles.

After a motorist moved past the recreation grounds, the road made a dip and continued into a descent for about two hundred and fifty meters, along which cops hid with radars to trap speedsters. Then the two-way street formed a junction with Mclean Boulevard, whose median separated the dual carriage way, that ran into Route 20 four hundred meters later.

That Wednesday morning, I got to the brow of the incline and saw a cop car with its front facing my direction. While I approached, a white cop moved toward the double yellow line in the middle of the way, and I identified him to be the one I had chased away a few weeks before in the park. The officer had his hands by his side, up to when I was about to pass the watchful pose he struck in the street. But he kept looking steadfast, cocking his head towards my windshield to keep me guessing that he might have wanted to see who was in the driver-seat. My tinted windows were up to make visibility difficult for the intruder.

Then it appeared he noticed my expired inspection sticker, and the hypocrite quickly held his hand out, telling me to pull over. Responding to his late signal, I couldn't brake up on time. So when I came to a halt, I had to reverse to obey his command.

"Is this your truck? You were driving at 41 in a 25 zone," he said. "Plus your inspection is out. Let me see your driving documents."

What a question, tendered at a time when he already knew he was about to review my particulars! As a black man, I must have committed a sin to be in possession of a property usually owned by privileged people. I knew my speed was not what he quoted, or else he wouldn't have waited that long to signal. I was pretty sure the reason he stuck his neck out was to check the inspection, and tacking on the speed section was his way of killing two birds with one stone. For, traveling over 40 down that grade would have thrown me headfirst into the blind traffic on Mclean Boulevard to be eaten alive. Anyway, I learned not to argue with a cop, especially when my hand was in the lion's mouth. Hence, after presenting him with his request, I sat in the vehicle and waited.

He gave the papers to his second sitting in the emergency tracker, while he must have broken the pace of about another ten violators to make them form a line. While his assistant did the ticketing, the trapper remained in ambush, and I observed the ample time the zapper gave each motorist, once he was sure they were speeding.

He later returned my belongings, along with two tickets without any further explanation. Which made the whole act look more like a highway robbery, where a group of guilty and innocent individuals were held up at gunpoint and shaken out of some cash.

I had had a perfect driving record until then - zero accident, no speeding ticket - and that was after being in the business since 1986 in different parts of the globe. When I drove off that morning, my day ended before it started, and I was in no mood to give my best in front of some adult students who were kids at heart. The tickets became a burden every time that I remembered the officer's attitude and the way he handled my situation. During my break, it grieved me to even look at them, but I did, and suddenly spotted the evidence that confirmed my speculation about the crooked cop. He recorded my speed as 43 instead of the 41 he initially brought to my attention, which put the guesswork into his game. I decided to contest it in court.

The courthouse in Paterson was perhaps designed with minority in mind. Security was tight all the way from the outside of the building to the interior, unlike the neighboring Elmwood Park location, which had the appearance of a castle than a place to spot convictions. Besides, the Paterson Police Station was part of the complex housing the litigation procedural department, as if to provide extra eyes for added protection - no trust impended. Positioned at the mouth of the town, the structure started with a glass-boxed entrance downstairs, manned by guards. That was unlike its extension in upper class Elmwood Park, where only a chiming bell sounded at the doorway to say someone entered.

Upstairs, benches waited patiently expecting a crowd, and on any given day, minority mothers suckled babies while biding their time to settle scores with the Court Office. When that wasn't the case, they were perhaps waiting on their friends or siblings to sign a bond to remove the handcuffs from the wrists of some felonious relatives. Inside the courtroom, the framed photos of a team of wigged magistrates decorated a conspicuous corner near the ceiling, but only one black face factored among the executive crop.

The court was scheduled to begin at 9 a.m. but at a quarter to the hour, the prosecutor appeared along with a host of lawyers running around like sharks and barracudas at the sight of blood in some surrounding waters. The fierce competitors must have been among those sending unsolicited mails to me, as early as a day after I had gotten those invitations from the squire.

Then the name-calling prosecutor welcomed those who had legal representation, while those without waited for eternity. Regardless of the severity of the appearance, someone without a lawyer had to make plans to kill the day in a very hostile environment. Then he had to hope for the best that he might hear his name, after listening to criminal cases. Or, after the judge took thirty minutes in the bathroom to clear his head of some mind-bogging misdemeanor case that he spent the whole day cracking.

But while all that took place, the prosecutor beckoned individual violators, and whispered a plea deal in their ears. Everyone signed to pay an additional four or five hundred dollars, to prevent their license from accumulating points along the normal route, which could lead to an eventual suspension. And it begged the question, what happened to those delinquents found wanting in dough to pay what they owed? Nevertheless, when it was my turn, it was a different jar of pickle.

"You pay five hundred and eighty-five dollars, and you can forget about points," said the public servant, holding the papers prepared for me to sign.

That was the big damage that the little difference between 41 and 43 had the potential of doing, and I wasn't going to have it.

"I want a trial," I said, feeling like I was acting out *Boys In The Hood*.

"Are you sure?" He looked at me like he thought I was a mad man. His tone changed as if to attempt to regain his authority that had actually slipped a little, when he spoke under his breath in his effort to consummate the contract.

"I want a trial," I repeated.

"Do you need an attorney?" asked the prosecutor, as if to say, if I didn't pay one way, it would have to be done in another.

From that instance, the mediating personnel appeared to perceive me as *Public Enemy Number One*, and to administer that enigma he stacked my plaint at the very end of the pile. When the magistrate finally called my name at mid-day, it was to communicate that Peter Griffin, the issuing cop, would be summoned for the next hearing to be held three months later on June 12.

After enduring equal waiting periods, I attended three more sessions without Peter's presence, and it seemed like a notation was made on my writ that I was a bad egg. For, the prosecutor could be having a good day until I faced him, and the whole mood changed. First, he asked if I wanted the same compromise that he offered from day one, while his eyes roamed the bottom end of the folded document that kept him up to date with my history. Then his jaws dropped to give me the idea that he remembered me from somewhere. Thereafter, I went through the same distressing wait until the end of the session, when the judge took my paper from the back of the pack and delivered his directives.

"If Peter doesn't show up the next time, your case will be dismissed," said the last presiding magistrate.

However, Peter and his working pal appeared in court for my next visit.

"Do you have an attorney?" asked the black judge, a switch from the usual white or Hispanic ones that I had faced in former times.

"No," I replied.

"Are you ready?"

"Yes."

"Are you sure?" It was as though the judge knew from experience, that nobody with my kind of wager walked out a winner, and that I never stood a chance if all I was relying on was to speak the truth.

The case was a year old, and I wondered how Peter was supposed to remember the whys and wherefores of what happened, having supposedly dished out perhaps thousands and more similar to mine since then. Of course, he had expected that everyone was just going to send a check in the mail, and his boss would have given him a raise for meeting the monthly mark.

Now that I had given him the shock of his life, how was he supposed to give a good account of what transpired? If the judge sat on his throne and believe every word Peter said, he would have sold the case as an acute instance of conspiracy. And that was seemingly the same vein in which the story developed.

"Describe your radar equipment and the last time they were checked." The judge was obviously building a case for the officer, establishing that Peter was not working with defective apparatus. However, I never doubted those tools for one minute; I had a problem with the crook's workmanship - his integrity to be exact.

The blind could see where this was heading, and I should have been less optimistic in believing that I could convince this black judge that the white officer was not to be trusted. Especially when the prosecutor denied my request to separate the writs after I pleaded guilty to 'failure to inspect'.

When it was my turn to talk, it was like the onus was on me to prove the equipment wrong. And every other word out of my mouth was met with the same intimidating tactics that I had observed to be at work, when the judge and prosecutor teamed up to project simple road violators as hardened criminals.

Then the magistrate told me to shoot questions at Peter.

"Since you knew I was speeding, why did you wait that long to stop me, so much so that I had to reverse because of your late signal?" I asked, just in time to see Peter change colors like a chameleon.

"Objection," said the prosecutor, "the officer did not say that in his report."

Was it too late to ask Peter if that had really taken place? I could never say that the cop lied about the late command, considering that he was not given a chance to respond. Besides, it could have been a case of lack of memory, or even deliberate omission. But the magistrate failed to use this against him, given that the prosecutor quickly swept it away.

"I find you guilty as charged," said the judge.

That verdict never came as a surprise, based on the way things were shaping up. But I questioned how a magistrate couldn't see the daylight that was visible in his sentence.

I took a part of the blame, bearing in mind that I used a half-truth after I realized Peter was dishonest in his recount of the incident. When the judge had asked how fast I believed I was traveling, I told him twenty instead of late twenties. But I exaggerated to confirm my susceptibility as a slouch, a characteristic that kept me accident-free during my driving history.

I left the courthouse feeling pissed off about America, and I began to slowly uncoil out of my dream like a pupa changing into a butterfly. I would have given anything if I could have flown back to my original state in my homeland, but my wings were clipped. I wished I could warn others that not everybody got it right in the land of black people's plight, and only a few did so while going to and fro.

CHAPTER EIGHT

My Foolish Advice

"Hello, hello! Yes Bruce. You wouldn't believe me if I told you I just got a three-month US visa," cooed Coolie, a longtime friend.

Poor Jamaicans! They had come to need visas for everywhere. At one point in time, when someone mentioned 'visa', it was taken to mean for USA only. Sometimes Canada. All of a sudden, that word needed a coefficient to avoid confusion.

Coolie rang to give me what he thought was glad tidings, but I was footing it all the way from town along the one-way portion of Park Avenue in the skin-consciously hot weather, just minutes after my court case. And anybody could just imagine my mood at that inopportune moment, though I didn't heave off my discomfort on my caller. It was strange but true that when folks called from Jamaica to America, they always expected great things, while the converse was in the affirmative for the connection vice versa.

"You're kidding!" I said, without realizing that his glee was about to be my downbeat guaranteed. I would have loved to think I didn't have to specify everything that I had been through, which was the perfect reason that many people back home found it hard to construe that America was really the land of make-believe.

"I need your help. Could you assist with my ticket? I can explain later." Coolie got straight to the point like he thought New Jersey was just another section of *The States* that had streets paved with gold.

That was when I felt compelled to give him my take on the trip that he eagerly awaited. I didn't know where to begin, but I had to say something, and my latest milestone gave me some meat on which to chew.

"I am just coming from court, and this system is not for people like us," I warned. "It's better to stay where you are and operate a taxi service, for example," I said, feeling like I was just uselessly gambling with words.

For, telling that to a thirty-six-year-old, pecking-order deejay with twelve children and a common-law, twenty-two-year-old, jobless girlfriend to feed was like throwing a straw, perforated basket in the deepest part of the ocean to give a drowning man. Even a rotten-rich guy would be hard-pressed to keep such a big catch together, and if Coolie couldn't keep his sanity, it was an understandable understatement.

He had been trying to make it in music since he took life into his own hands from the tender age of twelve. That was when he traveled the island on trucks to showcase his talents on platforms here and there. But that opportunity knocked whenever the emcees let him chant, as payment for lifting sound boxes and other heavy equipment. And now he sounded convincing that he would do anything to spread his wings elsewhere, like a disoriented and desperate disciple casting his net on the other side of the sea, after being forever faced with futility.

"Look, if you're going to help me, I prefer to see it in action," he said, making me feel guilty that I wasn't being the friend in need, like I was supposed to, on such a 'wondrous' occasion. It wasn't everyday that a conman look-alike in Coolie's category got up out of the right side of his bed to be so lucky with the American consulates, without consequentially owing some magician a fat lot.

If I didn't jump to his assistance, how was I supposed to live with the idea for the rest of his miserable life, knowing that according to him, I would have helped to prevent a good friend's progress? Nevertheless, I tried everything else, to see if he would reconsider under the premise of some other detriment.

"So what about your woman? What does she have to say about all of this?" I enquired, trying to find someone who could talk some sense into Coolie's head, concerning his precipitous plunge, even if the babble were for the wrong reason.

"Tanya doesn't decide for me," he remarked. "I am the breadwinner, and I make my move whenever I want, however I wish." Of course, I completely forgot that that part was nothing pertaining to the American culture where women had the last word.

If Coolie could only listen to himself! Tanya tried to persuade him not to yield to the same temptation that had destroyed so many families when the males separated to start a long distance romance. She was so madly in love with her man that within their four-year friendship, she delivered two children for him, and was three months on her way with their third when she suffered a miscarriage. Now, all of a sudden, picturing herself in the same position of many mothers who endured years without their husbands, was pointing her to the beginning of a chapter that was prime to exact its own toll on her whole life.

She cried day and night, went on a hunger strike, and hoped that Coolie would rethink his resolution, but instead, he thought she was losing her mind. He took her to a seer to find out if the devil was gaining on his lovely lady, and then to a church to ask a pastor to put in a word of prayer on her behalf.

Mom knew best, hence, Coolie relocated his missus like she was the old lady who lived in a shoe, to take up residence at his immediate family-house in St. Thomas. If everything went according to plan, that was where he wanted her to stay under mom's watchful eyes while he cruised the world.

Coolie's cooler wasn't going to get in his way, and neither was I. I gave him my word that the plane ticket would be bought and paid for at Newark Airport, and that he could collect it in Jamaica to meet his preparation to travel. The rest was up to him to ascertain that everything was decided in some deliberate order.

I took time from work to fight the afternoon traffic to reach the Air Jamaica travel agency at the flighty aircraft dispatch terminal. The day was hot and sticky and even carrion crows kept their distance somewhere less humid. Children splashed in the water from open fire hydrants all over town, as the gush hastily wormed its way along lucky sidewalks, before cascading into drainage tunnels.

Finding the entrance to the airport was one thing, but securing a place to park was quite another. The signposting was not easily fathomable, and I found myself in wrong lanes a couple times before I finally got it right, driving carefully along a winding road that took me to the top of a three-floor parking lot. After marking my spot among the thousands of other sparkling, stationary vehicles, I had to take the elevator two stages down, where I got help to find the pertinent office.

Once at the ticket counter, I described the kind of arrangement I desired, and based on my prior research, the attendant worked with the proper program to put me on the right track.

"Total cost is seven hundred dollars," said the female agent in glass-bottle-type lenses that gave the impression, she was as blind as a bat without them.

In retrospect, after I had discussed the fare on the phone, I thought I had the exact cash stapled together as seven one-hundred-dollar-bills, ready to be delivered right there on the spot. However, there might have been eight of them, and being fresh from the mint, two of the razor-edged ones remained stuck together like birds of the same feather.

When I refreshed my memory, trying to account for the missing money after my round trip through the traffic, it dawned on me that when the ticketing agent flipped the notes with her fingers, she quickly cut the count after the fifth stroke. Apparently, that was perhaps when she was satisfied that there was more of the triple-digit paper cash than expected, and moved to quicken my departure to keep it on the down-low. I came up with that possibility about the passed bucks a few hours after my return from the airport, at which point, it was pointless to cry foul play with any degree of plausibility.

On August 3, Coolie arrived in Connecticut, which later proved to be the beginning and the end of his endeavor. Actually, he had acted on an invitation from a crooked corporation to attend the festival that wasn't, in an attempt to see what could be patched up out of his shabby music mania. And once he had a foot in the country, the plan was to be all that he could to materialize his American dream.

Candy was this white American behind the brazen brainchild belonging to her and three other members of the organization. And though she was married, Coolie was hoping to see what good could come out of Nazareth, in the event that she had an agenda with him in mind. Candy and her phony personnel promised on paper to provide him with the first few days' accommodation, just so that he could slide past immigration and waltz his way into the garden of paradise.

At the makeshift concert, he could say a few lines on stage but he shouldn't expect a salary. And depending on how things went, he might need to pack his bags immediately after the show, like he had just been booted from *Beauty And The Geek*. He couldn't sign to these verbal agreements, but since he must have greased a few palms to get this far, there was nothing he could do to reject the indecent proposal at a later stage.

His personal producer was like a pimp in the partnership, and was pushing the pledge from an undisclosed location, watching the fireworks in the distance.

"I have spent millions on Coolie all these years, and I think it's time someone else picks up the mantle," said Mat.

Mat was perhaps one of many promoters that saw something glittering in Coolie as someone who could make it big in the industry, and the money-craver went after the talent like a Don King cashing in on a Mike Tyson contract. Coolie on the other hand, recognized the mosquito instincts in these predators, and took his stance like an Iraqi holding a gunpowder matchstick over some oilfields, ready to strike when the chips were not up in his country's favor.

According to Mat, Coolie was more like the wasp, in the story often told to explain why the flying insect couldn't yield honey, in spite of getting a one-on-one lesson from the maker. In other words, when one producer took the musical man under his wings, and reached the point where the talented artist could build the 'honeycomb', the deejay looked for the slightest opportunity to bolt in the other direction, bringing all efforts to a close, before he got the hang of reaping the sweet.

I was simply trying to find out more about the shaky arrangement on Coolie's itinerary in a very unforgiving place, knowing that a failure could find me in the midst of the confusion unexpectedly - like the case of the untimely ticket. Perhaps the only consolation was that Mat's mother was living in Yonkers, and could become useful in the case of a backfire. Banking on that kind of backup was not necessarily a shrewd option, by the way, bearing in mind that people in the USA hadn't yet surpassed the two-week unwritten law, that disallowed houseguests to overstay their welcome.

Before long, Coolie was homeless like he had charged into a brick wall, after which he sobered up to the reality that unlike Jamaica, he couldn't run next-door to get even a cup of water for free. He bounced from Hartford, Connecticut to Yonkers, New York, where Mat's mom tentatively took him in at short notice. Doreen was however taken by surprise, and couldn't forgive Mat for putting her up as reference, to corner her into something that seemed very fishy, when half of the tale had only been told.

Doreen didn't like the color of Coolie's money, considering that he had this thuggish appearance and streetwise approach to living, not to mention the fast lane to success that he cherished. A widow in her late sixties, she refused to remarry, channeling all her efforts into her own beautification. Mat was her firstborn and in his forties, but she had two other sons, all three within a four-year age-range of each other.

One would have been tempted to think that sharing a house with this grandmother of six, Coolie would have kept his lustful eyes off the woman who could have easily been his mother, all things being equal. However, a dozen kids with seven different gals should perhaps have provided enough proof, that Doreen shouldn't trust closing both eyes while sleeping under the same roof with such a guy. Under those conditions, Coolie was definitely like the fox put to watch the henhouse. And Doreen was glad to pitch him out in the streets, after she spent two weeks walking on eggshells in her own three-bedroom house.

Sex was sure going to be Coolie's downfall that it was unpredictable how his musical pitch was supposed to shoot for the stars. When he cut all contacts with Mat and Doreen, claiming that like mother like son, and that they had screwed him over from the beginning, he scrolled down his diary to fish for his next unfortunate victim.

He came up with Justin, who lived with his girlfriend in a studio flat in Springfield Close, Queens. From the get go, Toni was not pleased with her fiancé's arrangement to have Coolie sleeping on the living-room couch for even a night, much less any extended period.

"You've moved in a stranger," she complained, "and I don't know how much more of that I can take."

"Just wait Baby, please. Coolie and I have a history that dates back to our childhood," assuaged Justin. "Everything will soon be okay, I promise."

Toni wouldn't have known the story of their boyhood, since the couple only met in America, while he was a security guard at the J F Kennedy Airport, and she had lost a luggage on a flight one weekend. On the contrary, he and Coolie were in the same class in elementary school, and kept a close friendship into adulthood. Coolie's kids looked forward to Justin's regular visit to Jamaica, when they enjoyed the goodies that their Uncle Jus brought back for their merriment.

The cool guy's welcome came to a climax when Justin went to Canada and left him to be the man of the house during a best friend's absence. Justin expected Coolie to rule the roost, making sure that Toni felt safe until all three saw each other again in two weeks. However, one rainy afternoon, Toni arrived home earlier than usual to find Coolie having sex with a stranger on the only bed in place.

"What do you think you're doing?" Toni yelled.

"Please forgive me, it's been a long time and I was tempted," Coolie begged, while the stripper he picked up off the street sat naked on the ruffled, floral sheet, looking like a deer caught in a headlight.

"Is this what you do every day?" Toni asked, her mind dashing off in every direction, to imagine that for the past five nights, she might have been mingling in the mess created by these two extremists.

Coolie searched Toni's eye contacts to figure out if she was turned on by what she saw, desperately hoping that she might will her invaders to continue where they left off, in her efforts to join. He was thinking about everyone getting in that *when-the-cat's-away* kind of mood! All on board, they would all keep it a dark secret from Justin by the time it got around to his return. Notwithstanding, perhaps if it were only for the latter, Coolie could have stayed, but Toni was definitely not going to have it.

The rolling stone started having greater feelings for getting married to get his resident status, an age-old concept that had done its days. Almost every woman knew the trick, and had developed different set of rules like a bacterium coating itself with toxins to get the upper hand of antibiotics. Meanwhile, the government posed its own impediments not taking any prisoners, and if anyone believed that Coolie's ploy was anything new, he could be better off planting seeds in his homeland. First, a wife had to have the wherewithal to file for a man she went out of her way to call her husband. And second, she had to be employed, which ruled out drug traffickers and those on benefits, welfare or otherwise.

By some sordid twist of fate, Coolie came in contact with a married, man-controlling black-American bimbo, and the drama in his life unfolded further downhill. She didn't work except juggling marijuana, not learning anything from her record of being in and out of jail, leaving her kids to cry like baby chicks mourning the loss of mother hen.

The husband in her house lived like a mouse from the day he placed the ring on her finger, trying to shake the Dominican monkey from off his back, in his quest to become an American. That was fifteen years before, but in more modern times, someone in his right mind would have understood that Mrs. Janice St. Johns was an accident waiting to happen. Coolie couldn't see that this lascivious loser had a thing for Caribbean men, and as long as she got them in bed, she didn't have anything further to do with their carc*ass*. Hence, he lived on the empty promise that she was going to divorce the caged caveman, and marry him as her more recent sex slave.

And so Coolie moved in on the side, sharing the couple's matrimonial home located in a *project**, where his thirty-eight-year-old stalker raised a family consisting of an early teenaged daughter and a younger son. John, as her husband was called by his shortened surname, couldn't say a word when his rival was around, unless the timid rat wanted to end up behind rails like those other times, when his in-house accuser cut herself before calling the cops to deal with his case.

After a while, when it wasn't a friction between Janice and John over the presence of her live-in lover, it was a row involving Janice and Coolie over not fulfilling her promise to divorce the stumbling block. Although the female player was a tough trick, the Jamaican was the most formidable in the triangle. And the woman's kids got accustomed to being witnesses to a man they barely knew, choking and battering their mom in a neighborhood that was never deficient of such excitement.

Naturally her children took her side, but then came the makeup after the breakup, and the little ones were told to back up.

"Stay out of this," Janice ordered, when she remembered the rough sex that Coolie delivered, the night he sneaked in the room while everyone was fast asleep.

Both had grown accustomed to this lifestyle, and since she knew very well that after he had been on the run for a week or so, he normally made his sudden appearance, she made sure to leave his space vacant. The youngsters, on the contrary, just didn't understand the mind games their mom played. They woke up the next morning to sense another presence in the house, and greeted the disdain with disapproval.

Then Janice put her foot down like a diva, disregarding the abuse as if to say she wholeheartedly embraced the slogan, 'no pain no gain'. Nevertheless, she seemed to hope that some day, she would live to pay back evil for evil with something similar to the doses she meted out to her Dominican cuckold.

It must have been a good few months that I hadn't seen or heard anything from Coolie, and I thought that everything was going 'well' in his corner. After all, nobody had time to pay attention to anything else, except bills, and the means by which they were going to be paid. If I didn't hear from someone living in the USA, I took that to mean that he was busy doing whatever it took to survive. By then however, it was Tanya who was left on tenterhooks to figure out why she hadn't been hearing from Coolie, while the twelve kids in her care were living on borrowed time.

"I am only twenty-two years old," she reminded me, "and I shouldn't have to be left in this lurch," Tanya rightfully continued.

"I'll find out for you. Give me some time."

The tri-borough states enjoyed a state of perfect weather, unlike the week before when the humidity and heat index put ozone-related concerns in the hearts of those who worked in the open. It was a midweek change for the better, when the cool Canadian air swept in from the north, to give the great outdoors the best summer conditions one could ever anticipate. Those who had no immediate plans to put in more labor on their timesheets, horsed around in parks all over the place, while many working the normal eight-hour shift, watched the clock to join the frolic later in the afternoon.

I called the last number I had for Coolie and after much waiting, Janice picked up. The ambience wherever she was, could easily be mistaken for a midnight setting, surrendering to the interspersions of sleeping sighs. Besides, it was midday, but surprisingly the idle woman was still in bed while she dozily questioned me, as if that was too early to interrupt her daily routine.

"Who is this?"

"Bruce Welds."

"Oh, hi Mr. Welds. I've heard so much about you," she said in a very seductively sleepy voice.

"Is Coolie there? His kids need him."

When she heard about her bigamous boyfriend's strings that were attached to his coattail cross-ocean from Fletchers Land, it was as if she had just been drenched with a dose of poison. The jealous *Yankee* immediately smelled Coolie's baby mama, and her whole mannerisms changed in the instants before she put Coolie on the spot to defend his position.

The bitching brawler began to let off a lot of steam in the background, putting the deadbeat dad under pressure to prove that he had indeed broken up with Tanya before leaving Jamaica. Now, it appeared that although Janice had never met Coolie's trailer of troubled children in person, her animalism had installed the most recent version of an aversion for even the suckling that her new lover had left behind, way over yonder.

When Coolie took over, I detected that his behavior had reacted to the change of pace in the room, where he had stealthily kept a low presence, until those moments before his promiscuous partner got the disturbing message. He guarded his tongue while he spoke like he was lying beside an alligator that would snap him in two, if he ever made the grave mistake to leak certain information.

When he hung up, she went to use the ladies' room, and he escaped outside to buzz me back, so that he could speak his mind on a prepaid cellular phone that she had purchased to keep him in check. The wind was audible in the background, and each step he took along the pavement heading towards the train station, made his voice fluctuate on impact. He talked on top of his voice, lowering it when he suspected that someone might have been on his trail. And I sensed whenever he looked over his shoulders to ensure that Janice wasn't eavesdropping, or watching him from behind the drapes of her window upstairs.

That was how I realized that he was mad with me for looking after his children's interest. According to his foolish plan, he was taming the croc to take away her eggs, but for experienced people like someone living in the USA for some time, that wasn't going to happen without the hunter losing an arm or even his life. I hoped that the day would come when he would understand that he was sacrificing his children's birthrights by sticking around a helpless, married woman. He was actually getting flashes of that fact in his consciousness, but like a dream that winked at one's memory while the person was awake, Coolie was in the midst of the couple's life one day, and out of it the next.

A lot of theatrics went down before my compatriot came to his senses, at which time Janice refused to let go without a fight. By then, I had gotten a little more involved in the madness, finding accommodation for this man, who had pushed me to invest in his voyage.

However, the new living space didn't stop the stupidity from reigning in his brain. That which made him disappear two or three weeks at a time, to lock himself away with a sleaze, in a room where drapes hide the day from entering the infidel's apartment. It was not like he never had a choice to use Lincoln's recording studio, where the owner was deceived by the same optical illusion that pushed Mat to lay down 'millions' in Coolie's investment like a Wall Street stockbroker.

The next time anybody saw him, it was either that he and Janice had the usual fallout over failing to follow up with her divorce promise, or she just went berserk when he bragged about his kids. Both knew how to push each other over the edge, but while Janice was in her natural habitat, living like a bimbo pussycat, Coolie had too many irons in the fire, and needed to beat one while it was still red hot.

The back and forth of the starring actor might have been churning up in the USA, but in Jamaica, Tanya had been constructing an Oscar-winning cast on her own initiatives. She had had enough and told herself that her face was never booked by that *Godzilla* look. Then she got the courage to desert the home where Coolie subjected her to become a child again under his mother's roof. Since he wasn't sending anything to feed his army, somebody had to do it, and how about another man!

Tanya became tired of stressing out her mother-in-law in quotations, and found this guy, who was more than willing to step in to assist. Meanwhile, Grandma Maggie could only take so much and no more of Tanya's two-timing tactics, and decided to let her son know where he stood. When Coolie got the news, he felt like he was the Apostle Paul, struck by a bolt on his way to Damascus.

"Tanya, is it true you have a man?" he asked, hoping she would deny the allegation. But she stayed silent.

The bad boy loved Maggie, but not enough not to take his woman's words conveniently over his mother's to calm his jittering nerves. He preferred to hide from the truth, since he was too far away from the kind of action that would normally have pushed him to manhandle the young girl to get her back in line. His first inkling was that she had the kids to think about, and wouldn't just throw away everything, now that her man was in *The States*.

Then Coolie managed to put together a little something to send along with a wedding dress, and a pair of Cinderella shoes that he bought from *David's Bridal*. That package was supposed to reassure Tanya that she was still the wife, and even after a year, nothing had changed regarding their affair. And so, he continued to speak from both sides of his mouth, while his phone bore the evidence that he was an opportunistic player in practice.

A sixth sense told Janice that Coolie wasn't playing fair, and one night while he was sound asleep, she rummaged through his phone and found Tanya's number. She couldn't wait for the opportunity to confront her opponent.

"Hello, is this Tanya?"

"Yes it is." Tanya was not sure about the voice, but all that was about to change.

"Well, you don't know me, but I know everything about you. And that includes the fact that you're a ho**, and bitch, you need to get on with your sorry life. Coolie isn't coming back to you, so get used to the idea from now. I am his new wife."

Tanya didn't say a word, but called me to confirm the truth in what she just heard. I didn't want to be any more a mediator than what I had already been brainwashed to become, and I told her to get it straight from the horse's mouth. She apparently had better things to think about, but felt glad that the news gave her more power to blame the man in the middle for causing her to stray.

Strangely, Coolie's composure was never the same, though he covered his head in the sand when he heard that his family was falling apart. The thing that ate him out underneath like an underground erosive stream, was the grapevine news that Tanya had rented out the wedding gown, and had worn the 'hot-stepper' shoes to a party with her new beau.

If someone had told me that this guy's tough body was built with tear-glands like other human beings, I would have said 'go to hell'. However, when I overheard him crying like a bitch over the phone, talking to Tanya's mom who lived in Canada, I had faith in the possibility that even a lion could be tamed.

"I have everything ready here," he wailed. "By next year I should be there walking her down the aisle. She's my wife, Lola. Believe me! I am just here to make life for all of us. Do you think I like it in America?"

And after that, the once bombastic kid lost touch with his focus, and began to behave like Huckleberry Finn. Janice was making her own demands, and he was scooping up her assertiveness like his life depended on what came out of her mouth. During the good times, when they role-played their tension towards one another, she often told him that she would make sure that he didn't hit stardom, for fear that other women would get in the way.

And his head swelled to accommodate the trash talk, boosting his ego that she was spitting out something a woman in love usually said to lubricate her hormones in equilibrium. At that point, anything was expected from Coolie, not counting out the possibility that Janice might twist his arm to convert him into her partner in crime on the drug scene.

Fall had stepped in and the colder half was causing a stir, especially in the public's wardrobe. The dried leaves that littered streets and lanes were well parceled in black garbage bags, stashed away for collection. Squirrels sought nuts to stock up for winter, and skunks squirted perfumes to stimulate people's sense of smell.

As confused as he was, Coolie had drawn a little closer to the warmth that a woman could whip up, and he went missing for longer periods. He probably had enough sex to share, so that another gal from Yonkers was also getting some. His heart was still in Jamaica and according to him, he was only in it to win it - that is, anything these kinky tramps had to offer, from a pin to an anchor. At times, he stole their jewelry and even their underwear, (if he thought Tanya would look better than those *cows* wearing them), and loaded the loot in a traveling bag waiting for the gorgeous occasion.

Meanwhile, Janice got the symptoms and kept a close watch, though she couldn't put a finger on where the unsolicited help with her homework emanated. As for Tanya, Janice gave her a lead on life with that indispensable piece of advice, convincing her to look out for herself. But Coolie couldn't calm down, knowing that another bull invaded his pen. Every now and again, the sore loser displayed sporadic outbursts, bellowing and licking his wounds to show that he wasn't man enough to give and take. Sometimes he even forgot that there was no second chance for a man of his complexion in many parts of that borough.

It was one cold weekend in mid November, and Coolie had spent a few days well with Nina, the new woman in the picture. He had spoken to Janice that Thursday when Nina left for the pharmacy, and the former begged him not to stay away any longer. For that, the cheap trick promised to buy him a two-hundred-and-fifty-dollar coat and an expensive pair of sneakers, to be ready for him by the time he was back in the bed she had been denying her husband for her lover's sake. Of course, that was like showing candy to a baby, and Coolie couldn't resist the offer. So instead, he planned to spend the night with the sugar mom, before returning to Nina the next morning.

Not that Nina was a better buy when it came to women of class. She didn't work, and thought that her feces made the substance used to blend doughnut filling or ice cream flavors. Married, with a thirteen-year-old daughter to show from her separated husband, she drove a green Ford Explorer that she perhaps wrenched from some weakling, who fell for the ton of rear-end that pulled the rest of her body toward the ground.

Like Janice, she had something sugary to hold a Jamaican guy's interest. And for the moment, it was the settlement that she awaited to decide a divorce that was currently in the hands of the judge - something to that effect. The house was also up for grabs, and that was the interesting part that caught Coolie's neck in the noose. She filled his head with the idea that she planned to sell it, as soon as she was awarded the deal, which pretty much seemed to require that she only showed up at the starting line to pick up the podium prize.

Until then, it was Coolie who would have to do all the spending, though he didn't know where the next red cent was coming from to keep up the good work. Nina was enjoying the sex, and so both had something to lose if they pulled the trigger on each other's shortcomings. Right there, the code was established that she was the high maintenance mistress from the beginning, while he was the sex machine, no less than those the average big spender loved to entertain. But the big question was, how were they going to live it up without money?

The night the gigolo went to collect his freebies, he was hoping for a wham-bam-thank-you-ma'am easy access to the crocodile's nest. He performed his best as usual, but he watched the time with every tick of the clock. The morning worms were glowing in their hibernation, so there was no way to judge if Coolie beat the early bird to be on the rise. However, he was ready to sneak out at the slightest possible chance, if he could only slip from under Janice's clutching legs that she threw across his waist, half-covered under the comforter.

That break came after she took an early morning ride, while he lay on his back to make her feel in control. Then she slid off and rushed to take a shower, to be fresh to impress for a second round during the course of their relaxation. It was the change of stage Coolie was hoping for, and if he let that one slide, he might have to stick by her disgusting side for another night. He couldn't see himself in that situation.

While the shower curtain was drawn at full mast, and the scent of sweet gel escaped over the rod and into the room where they both had just finished their sex fete, Coolie quickly dragged on his suit that was hanging on the headboard. His new, black, leather coat was incidentally a great match. He then grabbed his overnight bag in which he had stuffed all his belongings that had manifested his presence in those controversial corners.

While Tanya was humming to the tune of *Amazing Grace*, she heard some movement at the door, but didn't think anything of it, least of all that that was going to be her last encounter with the devil. When she returned to the room, only the warm cover partially straddling the carpet, bore witness that she had had company the night before. Wearing just a transparent nightgown and a pair of bed slippers, she ran downstairs with a bottle of *Clorox Bleach* in her hand, suspecting that Coolie had taken off with the new outfit to visit some girl, who had text-messaged him a few seconds after he arrived overnight.

The sky was gray, but rain was nowhere in sight to give the countable commuters heading to catch the early train, any reason to carry umbrellas in panicking expectation. The atmosphere was getting stiff cold to match the reserved silence among those visible on the elevated platform, across from the cockroach-infested, six-story housing *project*. People simply rationed their speech while they melted down to meet the rest of the day.

Janice dashed towards the train station, reading her man's movement like a book. And sure enough, there he was, dressed to kill like a statesman. He was so focused on the phone talking to some *trailer trash*, Nina to be exact, unsuspecting that his tracks were uncovered, at least from Janice's direction.

"Where do you think you're going?" Janice shouted.

Coolie looked around and knew immediately that all hell had broken loose. He couldn't afford to fuel the uproar, since Nina on the line knew nothing about the melodrama, which was about to suck in everybody in its path like a hurricane.

"I'll be back soon," he tried to throw a catch at Janice, hoping she was too blind with rage to see the stopover bag in his hand. Meanwhile, he kept the receiver down against his leg to prevent the melee from reaching the wrong ears.

Janice saw red, as she grabbed onto the coat on her suitor's back to create a scene. But in order to prevent that, Coolie walked back to her car that was parked a few meters from the *project*, while she followed suit. They calmed down a little, after he gave her the impression that they could discuss their differences without taking the show on the road. She opened the car door, and both of them tumbled inside, panting like two pit bull terriers, rescued from a *Michael Vick's Dogfight* show.

They argued again and she spoke about the things she bought, discrediting him for his ingratitude and dishonesty. Tempers flared and a fistfight ensued when Janice opened the bleach bottle, to douse the coat that was partially causing the fuss. Coolie was just in time to intercept the liquid, manipulating it towards her naked crotch during the tussle. He fought off his challenger to hold his hand in place, emptying the gallon container into the bull's eye where he directed the dispenser, before grabbing his load and fled.

Someone must have called the cops, for they appeared like greased lightning to curtail his movement. Janice was understandably the last person to wish for an eye contact with the officers. And like an unarmed guy hiding in the closet while gunmen ransack the room, she had her heart racing up to her mouth in the presence of the law-keepers. Keeping a stiff upper lip, she downplayed the significance of the fracas to get them to leave, after they initially confiscated some of Coolie's particulars, including his phone.

The story was still not finished when Coolie left with his 'acid-wash' jacket, or when Janice walked back to her apartment with the most sensitive areas of her inner thighs dripping with the caustic solution. By the time she entered the shower, it was too late to prevent severe burns from penetrating her private parts, and so she had to seek medical attention.

"I am not going to suffer anymore in silence," she told me out of desperation.

We weren't the best of friends from the beginning, since I didn't support the ill-fated complications characterizing the unstable union. However, necessity suddenly became the mother of invention, and she thought I was the one in the best position to lend an ear. Hence, like a prisoner embracing everyone in freedom as his friends, the woman who once tore me to bits when I took up for twelve unfortunate Jamaican children, was now purposefully willing to divulge the lurid details that was about to destroy the dad of those same kids.

She pressed charges against Coolie, using the medical evidence, which stated that she suffered physical traumas to her body, and a warrant went out for the arrest of the illegal alien. The officers left a message on Coolie's voicemail, telling him to turn himself in at the Yonkers Police Station. He too should have been more careful to avoid looking in the eyes of the tigers, since he had put in to prolong his stay in the US, and was awaiting a verdict.

Not wanting to push his already bad luck any further, he went in hiding with Nina, perhaps hoping that the police would forget about him and pay attention to more burning issues. Meanwhile, he had no other choice than to come clean with his new missus, who for some reason, just slapped his wrist and stood by her man.

The heat was on, and he figured that if he called Janice for both of them to come to a compromise, the cops might simply mind their own business. But the snappish drug peddler decided to take her sweet revenge, especially when she remembered that another woman had become an extension of the equation. To cut a long story short, the police picked up Coolie after he made another call from a hotel room, where he was relaxing with Nina.

His latest lover was to the rescue, writing letters and sending money to his account, while he spent forty-five days in jail. Not that he really had a choice, when not even his closest friend could stand the twenty-thousand-dollar bail for his freedom. The preliminary part of his agony came to an end when the authorities carried out an investigation, and discovered that Janice had a history of abusing her kids, was a felon, and her rap sheet was complete with numerous counts of drug-affiliated charges and convictions. Consequently, Coolie was granted bail on his own recognizance, but was slated to return to court subject to notification.

Janice saw Coolie after the great showdown, and requested a happy reunion as if she had gotten over the burns, promising to drop the case if they both turned over a new leaf. If not, she could stay the course and see him back in court on December 28. With the first-gear of a good attorney, she could get him to pay for assault inflicting bodily harm, plus face deportation. However, despite having that dark cloud dangling over his head, Coolie and Nina had different plans that would soon swallow up that case like a Saddam Hussein falling through a deathtrap.

Though Nina lived in Yonkers, she originated in Connecticut where she worked in a financial institution during her early twenties. That was before her mirror played tricks on her brain, disillusioning her to believe that she shouldn't have to work that hard in real life. Then she viewed men differently, that they were supposed to serve one main purpose, and that was to make her happy by meeting her monetary demands. She showed her husband the door for failing that test, but vowed that the next guy to share her bed would also show the most merits in the above regards, apart from just good sex.

Nina must have watched too many action movies that spurred her to entertain the idea of self-promotion, to go from a bank worker to a bank robber. And that was where Coolie's tough-guy talents came in handy.

"Sometimes I feel like robbing a bank," he said that last Monday morning I saw him, after he took a quick run overnight to visit the little room that he didn't even have time to clean.

He had asked me for ten dollars in desperation, trying to make it back to Yonkers, but I refused to be a part of his carelessness. Concerning the bad urges that he expressed on that occasion, I thought he only said so to get some attention. But I still didn't have the silliest suspicion that he meant business, never mind where he got the notion. Except I figured Nina was behind it, since lately, he had come under pressure from her, after severing all ties with Janice.

I hadn't heard anything from Coolie even after December 28, and I thought he had worked out something to conclude his court case. But boy, was I wrong! I thought of the devil, and one day later my landline rang - it was he. However, the Caller ID registered that someone from a correctional facility was trying to contact me. At first, I thought Janice had stirred up a hornets' nest at Coolie's feet again, and immediately, I wanted to keep as far as possible from that kind of mud bath. The answering machine took the blow.

I listened as the automated speaker gave some options allowing Coolie to say his name, before specifying the conditions under which the contact could be made with the inmate.

"Inmate," I said loudly, with no one to correct me if I went wrong. It was only a few weeks before, I had accepted a few such calls because of Coolie's capture, and my phone bill for that period skyrocketed.

I regained consciousness after the phone rang in rapid succession, but I still decided against answering. I was therefore lingering in the dark, not knowing how he got back in prison, and I really didn't care. A letter arriving in the mail was supposed to clear that up in *his* own handwriting.

Nina and Coolie had driven to Connecticut on a bank-robbery spree, got away with the loot, and made it as far as heading south on the New Jersey Turnpike. It meant that they had cleared the crime scene, but just when they thought it was peace and safety, it was sudden destruction. They stopped to pay toll, and that was one wrong turn that detoured the devil and his angel on the road to perdition.

As they approached the booth, the female driver fitted the description of the one in the getaway vehicle that was in the hot seat of the nationwide search. Meanwhile, the two culprits were never at ease, fidgeting at the sound of worn rubber threads on the gritty tarmac as they neared, coming to a slow but suspicious halt, in spite of their pretentious image on the frontline.

The night was a reflection of pristine weather, with not even a cloud in the sky. Stars twinkled above, but no one saw them in light of the lampposts intermingling with the low beams of six or more trains of vehicles, that looked more like a magnified demonstration of bacterial cells. Some however, broke the chain and jostled through, courtesy of their *E-zPass* provision.

The officer in the cubicle where Coolie was chauffeured into dsifficulty by his daring prima donna, refused to lift the lid to let them through. But instead, the obese Russian-American closed the glass window, and picked up the intercom hanging on the wall next to his seat. Before the civilian-looking cop could finish, two uniformed lawmen moved out in front, and the red light appeared at the fore of the tollbooth's roof to declare lane closure.

The traffic behind Coolie and Nina began to drift to the other vacancies. Since nobody said a word to any of the two fugitives up to that point, Nina put the stick in reverse, as if she didn't realize she was the reason for the delay. She intended to follow the crowd crossing over to join the other lines.

"Don't move!" one of the officers instructed, and his radio was activated. "Stay seated with your hands on the dashboard," he commanded, while a million more men of order appeared out of holes, like rats invading the town of Hamlin.

The cops encircled the cars with high-powered weapons, while their eyes penetrated the parked SUV like flashing laser beams emitted from a control tower. Meanwhile, Coolie must have pissed his pants a thousand times or more, as he looked intently in the eyes of his companion, thinking about the seventy-eight thousand dollars in the bag that they couldn't touch under the backseat. It was so close, yet so far away.

The cash was recovered as Coolie was caught while his sticky fingers fused to the full amount, like a rat with its teeth in the cheese while its head was still in full clamp. Needless to say, he was sentenced to fifteen years in prison according to the terms of a federal crime. Nina was given a lesser penalty after she claimed she was coerced into the act, and being an American, plus a female one at that, what else did anybody expect?

Trouble came in twos and threes, and that was no superstition for Coolie. Back home, Maggie lost her oldest son due to a blood clot in his brain, and now she was pushed to face losing a second one to a penitentiary she couldn't even visit. I lost contact with Janice after her two lines went dead for good. And as for Tanya and her team, she simply joined the long line of ladies who lost their partners to traveling and its eventualities.

Coolie made himself at home among a band of hoodlums, some serving time for crimes they didn't commit, but rather based on reputation or skin-color. Others were guilty and got what they deserved. Whatever the reason for their inclusion, Coolie didn't have to become a pillar of salt in Sodom while his talent wasted.

Being a little more familiar with the story that captured headlines in local newspapers, I decided to accept a call from the bugger to hear how a big guy could come down as little as a fly.

"What up yow?" he greeted, laughing his head off as if he had recently landed a White House job.

I knew it had been a while since we hadn't spoken, and therefore he might have been glad to hear my voice. But his dilemma should have outdone that kind of joy, to prevent him from coming across as happy-go-lucky while his head was still in the vice. Besides, I had sacrificed time and money, for which I was sensing a lack of respect. Altogether, he was definitely taking my efforts for granted. For that I jabbed him with a clean body blow.

"Your brother is dead," I said, without dressing up the skeletons to cushion the effects. The line went silent, while he switched from a man exuding joy and pride to a voice demonstrating *Dr. Jekyll and Mr. Hyde.*

"What, what, what, ah, what did, did, did you say?" he stuttered, as if he had just been hit by a sledgehammer deservedly across his forehead.

Getting that kind of news in incarceration was like a new amputee slamming what was left of his leg against the floor, forgetting that he needed crutches all the more.

"He had a clot, and was buried two weeks ago. Anyway, I have to go." And I hung up to spare a hefty phone bill on my account.

Like I told Coolie in a letter, I had no time to lecture to anyone, unless I perceived where I could help saving that individual from the pangs of destruction. And while he was doing time, I couldn't do much for him without wasting precious moments, which was essentially what I loathed to a very great extent. I wasn't getting any younger, my American dream was still a far way off, and that pretty much said everything.

Coolie's prison term could have taught a good lesson to the two point five million Jamaicans, in population of the eleven thousand square kilometers of mountainous terrain in the West Indies. And that morale was, if Mr. Shark should announce from the deep that whales had scales on their hands and feet, it was best to take him at his words, even when he overwhelmingly seemed absurd. Coolie lived to pay the price refusing to take my foolish advice.

* *Project: a low-income housing scheme in the American inner cities*
** *American informal usage, meaning 'whore'*

www.ingramcontent.com/pod-product-compliance
Lightning Source LLC
Chambersburg PA
CBHW030503260626
47157CB00005B/1629